GW00385098

30130 069331485

The Landmark Library
No. 13

THE STORY OF RAGGED ROBYN

The Landmark Library

OLIVER ONIONS
In Accordance with the Evidence
The Story of Ragged Robyn
Widdershins

GEORGE MOORE
Celibate Lives
Conversations in Ebury Street

ARNOLD BENNETT
Mr. Prohack

T. F. POWYS
The Left Leg

MARGARET IRWIN
Still She Wished for Company

ANN BRIDGE
The Ginger Griffin

CHARLES MORGAN
The Gunroom

C. E. MONTAGUE
Rough Justice

FR. ROLFE
Don Tarquinio

T. H. WHITE
They Winter Abroad

S. BARING-GOULD
Mehalah

THE STORY OF RAGGED ROBYN

Oliver Onions

CHATTO & WINDUS

LONDON

Published by
Chatto & Windus Ltd.
London

*

Clarke, Irwin & Co. Ltd.
Toronto

First published 1945
This edition first published 1969

SBN 7011 1374 X

Printed in Great Britain
by William Lewis (Printers) Limited
Cardiff

TO

Jane Mary Clare Oliver

To-day, at this distance of time, we see these things as behind some thick horn pane, tallow-smoked and cloudy and intercepting as much light as it lets through. We read of waylayings and hamesuckens, or cruel threats and implacable redemptions, and wonder whether it was not better to have lived under the Danelaw outright than to suffer a 'protection' that no longer protected anybody. Little is known of this Peg Fyfe and her Holderness crew, and of young Robyn still less. It is not even certain that that was his name, so do the harmless names perish and the infamous ones survive. But here follows his story, pieced together from such fragments as remain.

I

YOUNG Robyn Skyrme, trudging along by the side of the sea-wall with his pack of tarred cloth on his back, was secretly glad of the feel of his pistol in his pocket. This was not because he heard anybody behind him, for on such a windless evening the smallest sound would carry for a mile or more, and nothing broke the silence but the complaining of the sea-birds, the shuffling and crunching of his own feet and the muffled jolting from the burden on his back. Nor was there anybody ahead, for the sea-wall ran as straight as a ruler, without as much as a bush for anybody to hide behind. But each moment the wall was showing its edge more sharply against the failing light, there was a path along the top of it, and by climbing up its slope he would be able to see all around him at once. As the weight of his budget threw his balance out for climbing he unshipped it from his back, thrust it up first, clambered up after it, and then proceeded to buckle it to his shoulders again.

From the top of the wall his view was much more extensive. That faraway whispering on his right was the sea, lost in the in-creeping night-fret, out of which a misty midmoon showed no more yet than half its horn. Inland, too, were thin earth-vapours, intercepted by the long lines of the dikes that reflected back the fading sky. That was why the wall was there, for with a spring tide and a north-east wind to drive it all that side sometimes became a waste of tumbled water, drowning the cattle and washing away the stacks and making a desolation for miles round. Then everybody had to turn out, men and women and young Robyn too, to mend the breached wall again.

His errand that afternoon had been to the Saltings, and the pack on his back held what was always spoken of as 'the medicines'. These were landed at the Saltings on certain dates because of the creek and the tides, but he had carried them a long way, his legginged feet caught in the tough sea-holly that grew along the wall-top, and though he was thirteen and strong he would be glad when the next three miles brought him home. For he was uneasily aware that the pistol in his pocket was not a real one. He had carved it out of a holly-root he had found one day, already so like a pistol that he had not been able to refrain from finishing it with his knife, even fitting a flint to its double-tooth of a hasp. But since then he had learned to read and write, and with six books of his own at home he had something more exciting to do with his evenings than carving wooden spoons and wheatears when somebody needed a new breadboard.

Between the lights, with the medicines growing heavier with every step he took, he continued to trudge along the wall-top, till the light died out of the west and over the sea the moon stepped out of her silver bath.

But against the afterglow on the landward side a strange shape suddenly appeared. Still distant, it was lifted above the earth to twice the ordinary height of a man, and it advanced stiffly and staggeringly, yet with unusual speed for all its clumsy gait. It was a fenman on his stilts, with his twelve-foot pole to steady him, and bobbing and dancing half-way up in the sky like that he had a gallows-like look, as if some malefactor from York Castle, swinging in his rusty hoops and shackles, had cut himself down for an evening stroll. And as this shape stalked steadily towards the wall Robyn remembered the medicines on his back and that his pistol was only a wooden one after all.

He was reckoning up the chances of a nimble lad on a wall against a grown man with only three stilts to prop him when the figure was on him. Even standing on the lower level he was still as tall as Robyn. But instead of taking a cut at him with his staff, he spoke after a friendly fashion.

'Bide a bit till I light my lantern,' he said, and propped up like a tripod he fumbled with flint and steel and tinder. Then he closed the shutter of the lantern, and as the candle-end became bright Robyn could see his face. It was straggly-bearded and elderly, and his brows were close and bushy, but the eyes underneath them were bright and harmless.

'And what might you be doing here at this hour?' he asked, while Robyn looked at the accoutrements with which he was hung, a sort of fowling crossbow or prodd, a quiver of short bolts, a length of rope and a large knife.

'Minding my own business,' said Robyn, not nearly as stoutly as the words sounded, and the fenman gave a nod.

'Good for you, captain. A very proper answer as times go, and you look a proper lad. Do you know who *I* am?'

'Not without you're Watty, the kempery-man,' and again the answer was approved.

'Good again. Never hold speech with those you don't know. Watty it is, though my kemping days are by. Do you know what a Dutchman's clout is?'

'No.'

'It's the one before the first, the same as you were thinking of giving me when I came up. What's that on your back?'

'Herbs,' said Robyn, to keep on the cautious side, and again he heard the chuckle.

'Ay, gathered at neap tide when Roger's hoy puts in. Herbs in jars and bottles from Holland and France. Well, saving we're outlaws, we're all men of peace now, and Roger's trade's as honest as another. Give me a hand over the wall. I'm getting on in years to be scrambling over walls in these stees o' mine.'

Robyn helped him over with the stilted legs. Then, when he was upright again on the seaward side of the wall, he suddenly glanced round and dropped his voice, as if there had been any but the seabirds to hear.

'I take it you're the lad from Unthank. I was coming round your way, but you can save me a few miles if you take 'em word. Did you hear what I said just now? "Barring we're outlaws," I said, and if there isn't a law in the land we've got to make one. Have you Unthank folk any news from Holderness?'

'No,' said the boy in a suddenly altered voice.

'No,' the man nodded, 'else they wouldn't have sent you as far abroad as this. Then you can tell 'em. Fifteen of 'em's been seen, making for Sunk Island. That was three days ago, and they'll have scattered beside, a few here and a few there, and they might be anywhere by this. How many are you at Unthank?'

'Nine, counting the women,' said Robyn in a lower voice still.

'Then tell John Skyrme to see to his doors and fastenings and prime his pistols. If you've cattle out at gistment get 'em in. A couple of you'd better sleep in the stable. Tell any you meet on the way, but only if you know who they are – or don't you know what I'm talking about?'

The boy's 'I know' was hardly audible.

'Then I'll be getting along to warn 'em at the Point. Get you home the gainest way, and keep your eyes open. If they can't make laws for us we must shift for ourselves, and good night to you. I wish you safe home.'

Inland nothing little now showed but the patchy vapours and the pale intersecting straight lines of the dikes. The half-moon, clear silver now above the fret, dimmed the kempery-man's lantern to a smoky glow as he straddled away. Dancing like a will-o'-the-wisp, it grew less and less, and then suddenly went out entirely. Robyn was left with only the moon for company.

2

HE began by whistling, for the old soldier had called him captain and said he looked a proper lad; but whistling needs the rhythm of a tread, and there is no advancing with confidence when you have your feet to watch at every step. Spurge and sea-holly grew along the wall-top, and the sea-holly was pale and witch-like in the moonlight, but every tuft cast a shadow, and presently his whistling died away. He had got up on the wall to be able to see all round him, but now it occurred to him not only that he could be seen himself, but that nothing could be more conspicuous against the moon-shot mists than the long straight line of the wall with himself advancing along it. If he got down on the landward side he and the wall would make one shadow, but any step might land him in a pool or hole. Better the other side and the moonlight, and there was no need this time to remove his pack. The jars in it made a knocking as, seating himself, he slid down again.

But even the getting down from the wall had made a difference. It wasn't that he had been afraid up there; nay, he must have had a bold, swaggering look, for the kempery-man had thought he was going to take a Dutchman's clout at him; but now he felt he must have something to occupy his thoughts. So he began to run over the afternoon's events again, the hoy lying on her side in the creek waiting for the tide, Roger whose trade was as honest as the next man's, his shore-agent, who knew them all at Unthank and had handed over the medicines without any question. But neither Roger nor the agent had said anything about Holderness. Holderness and its thieves was nothing to them, for if fifty of them had crossed over by Sunk Island, Roger would have been standing out on the tide for Antwerp again by that time. So Robyn suddenly set Roger on one side and tried to think of his six books at home instead.

The Bible, of course, came first; but the *Pilgrim's Progress* and the *Book of Martyrs* were not far behind. Then came the Herbal, which also had texts in it, as when young Reuben had found the mandrakes in the field and taken them home to his mother. But on none of these could he keep his thoughts fixed for more than a few moments. Why wasn't he at home, studiously reading them, instead of tramping alone by the sea-wall, and even Watty the fenman saying he ought to be safely under a roof, and bidding him get back there as fast as his legs would take him.

And that was the last of his pretending, for it was better to look it in the face. Watty, too, had a bed, but instead of getting into it he was going round on his stilts, telling people to get their beasts in from gistment and to prime their pistols and bolt their doors and set somebody to sleep in the stables. It was three days since they had been reported crossing by Sunk Island, and once on this side they would have scattered again, a few here and a few more there, ambushing the roads and not even the houses safe. And suddenly he fetched up short with half the breath knocked out of his body.

He felt the chill of the incoming fret about his knees; now at the slight dipping of the shore it was about his waist and thickening in a high bank before him. It was at that point that the Stakes began, and he had walked into the first of them without seeing it. Bruised and startled, for he had struck it with his face, he started back. Like a scattered plantation he could see them ahead, striped pine trees, some of them leaning over at angles, with their tops jutting up into the moonlight and tattered shreds of old fish-netting below. And that meant good-bye to the friendly sea-wall, for a little way past the Stakes it ended. After that the sour spurge and the witchlike sea-holly and other brackish herbage of the shore gave place to soft drifted sand, patched with scrub and tamarisk and thorn. It meant good-bye to the moon too, for with the beginning of the sandhills the cart-track to Unthank became a rough rutty lane, with over-arching trees, only the dim tops of which could be seen against the sky. And it was the thought of these trees that made Robyn do what he next did.

Drawing closer in to avoid the Stakes he reached the rampart of cobbles that brought him level with the wall again. Seating himself on these he again unstrapped the budget from his back. Of rum and brandy and fiery schnapps it had a jar of each inside it, and he knew these things were not for boys, but he had heard grown men speak of Dutch courage, and with a little extra courage he would be safely home. He felt for the jar with the least rammed-home cork, and out in the moonlight came his knife. With the cork in the palm of his hand he set the jar to his lips. He spluttered and choked, but forced the stuff down, and felt the red-hot track it left behind it. To make sure he had a second and this time a larger swig. Then, replacing the jar in the pack and the pack on his shoulders, he got on his feet and started forward again.

Five minutes later he was whistling as he had never whistled before. Never in all his thirteen years had he felt so lively and jaunty and brave. Whistling was not enough, so he began to sing instead. *Follow the Horses* he sang, which was a song Sim Dacres the head-hind had taught him. Over and over again he sang it:

> '*As me and my marrow was gannin' to wark*
> *We met with the devil, it was in the dark*—'

Corporal Watty had called him Captain and said he was a

proper lad. The pack was a featherweight on his shoulders. If he had had a stick he would have taken a Dutchman's clout at anybody, if his holly-root pistol had been a real one he could hardly have been more cock-a-hoop:

'So I up with my pick, it being in the neet,
And I knocked off his horns, likewise his club-feet—'

he sang at the top of his voice as he approached the clump of yew-trees that marked the beginning of the lane.

He saw no light, heard no sound. He was just beginning to sing again, 'I knocked off his horns,' when a rough hand was clapped over his mouth. His feet were no longer on the ground as he was hustled through a gap, and by the time they touched it again his arm had been given a rough twist and a scarf or bandage was being tightly fastened over his eyes.

After that all became a confusion of which he knew little. He was being hurried over short turf, which meant he was being taken in the direction of the sandhills. He had no idea how many his assailants were, nor was he any wiser when, some little time later, he was jerked to a standstill, for the loose sand muffled the footfalls and instead of his eyes being unbound his blinker was only made the more secure. A villainous voice sounded in his ear, and he started violently as the point of a knife touched his throat.

'Who are you, and what's your name?'

He was too terrified to reply, so this time the knife at his throat drew a little bead of blood.

'What's your name?'

'Robyn Skyrme.'

'Where through?'

'Unthank.'

'Is that the farm up the lane?'

'Yes—'

'How many horses have you there?'

As Robyn did not answer the point of the knife was again set to his throat, but suddenly a deeper voice took charge.

'Have done, Perkyn, and let me ha' a word with him.' This grimmer voice reached Robyn's ears, and even though he did not see the speaker, Robyn had the feeling that he was gigantic. 'Hark you, sonny. How old are you?'

'Thirteen.'

'And how old will that mak' you in another seven years?'

'Twenty —' said Robyn faintly.

'Have you ever heard tell of the Queen of Holderness?'

Robyn's dry gulp signified 'Yes.'

'I'm her son, the Prince of Withernsea, and I've brought you a message from her. Tell them where you belong their protection money's overdue and we're out collecting it. They'll know what you mean. To-morrow night, at this time, your four best horses is to be by those yew trees where we found you. My royal mother's orders is that they're to have halters and their feed round their necks. You're to bring 'em yourself, alone, and if you don't, or if you breathe a word about it to a living soul, you'll feel the weight of what she's got in her pocket.'

'Tell him what that is, Prince,' the other voice said.

'We won't say what it is, but let's say it's a stone she keeps for them that disobeys her royal commands. If she hasn't flung it at the end of seven years she spits on it and turns it over and puts it back. But it's always flung when the time comes, seven years or seventy.'

'Just remind him, Prince, and then tell him again in case he forgets,' and again Robyn felt the point of the knife.

'To-morrow night, at this time, by the yew trees. Your four best, with halters and their feed round their necks. And remember the stone, and that royal Queens doesn't say things twice. Now set him on his way.'

Somewhere near the yew trees the bandage was removed

from Robyn's eyes again. Robbed of his pack, seeing little more than he had seen when he had been blinded, and terrified lest that trickling at his throat should mean he was slowly bleeding to death, he stumbled drunkenly up the cart-track that led to Unthank.

3

THE beams and framing of Unthank had gone up in Elizabeth's day, and there was not a scrap of stone about the place, for its lower walls were of flints set in mortar, polished as bottle-glass and built to stand till the Day of Doom. But its upper part was of white cobbles from the beach, and when evening fell this whiteness gave it the look of a house floating in the air among its mistals and stables and other outbuildings of a large farm. Robyn's bedroom was in the small roof-chamber just under the belfry, where hung the bell that called the hinds in from the fields, but Robyn was late that night, and John Skyrme was beginning to fidget.

'He's a grown lad and knows the way home from the Saltings well enough,' Margaret Skyrme rapped back, for Robyn was no son of hers, but John turned to Sim Dacres, the head-hind.

'The wind's shifted since he left and there's a sea-fret. If he isn't back soon you'd best go look for him,' and he went upstairs to set a light in the window of Robyn's belfry-room, where it would be seen the farthest.

But another half hour passed without any sign of Robyn, and John Skyrme, having occasion to go round by the stables, looked in to see that all was well. He was about to leave again when he thought he heard a throaty, choking sound. It came from under the ladder that ran up to the loft, and he raised his lantern higher. There, on a truss of straw pulled down from the loft, lay Robyn, sick-drunk. Even when John Skyrme bent over him he made no attempt to get up.

'Why are you so late and what have you been doing?' the farmer demanded, for the smell of rum is a penetrating one and his brow had gathered. 'Where's your pack?'

The lad only shook his head stupidly. He seemed afraid to speak, and John Skyrme shook him and hoisted him to his feet. He could hardly stand, and again he was asked where his pack was. But the cuts on his throat were no longer bleeding, and all that John Skyrme saw was the straw in his disordered clothing, his hair like a tumbled cornstook, the freckles across the bridge of his nose and cheekbones and the frightened stupor in his blue eyes. For the third time he asked where his pack was, for now that the lad himself was safely home the medicines were no small matter.

'They took it off me.'

'Who took it off you?'

But scared to death that he had said even so much the boy did not answer.

For he was the bearer of not one message but of two. The one he brought from Watty the fenman was that Unthank was to bar its doors and see that its pistols and flintlocks were made ready; but the other was that if he breathed a word of these things to a living soul something dreadful would happen to him, though it took seven years in coming. He had no recollection of how he had got home. He only knew that he must have made for the stables rather than be seen by anybody in the house, and that he must have seized a pitchfork to take a Dutchman's clout at somebody, for it was still in his hand. But he must have slept a little, lying there on the straw, for his nausea was beginning to pass, and whereas John Skyrme smelt only the tell-tale fumes of the rum Robyn smelt the warm smells of the stable again, its straw-manure and droppings and stalings, its musty chaff and the corn in its bins. Watty had said it would not be amiss if somebody slept with the horses, but whoever did this would need a real pistol in his pocket, so Robyn had armed himself with a pitchfork instead.

'Who took your pack, and what are you doing with that in your hand?' the farmer demanded again, and at that his desperate idea of telling without telling was born in Robyn's head.

For in the nearest stall stood Starlight, and Robyn sometimes thought that next to the Bible and the *Pilgrim's Progress* he loved the mare better than he loved anything else in the world. She seemed to have been specially made for his weight and balance, a deep bay with stiff quarters and a hunter's head, and her coat was glossy with Robyn's brushing and her tail sleekly combed and breath sweet. She loved Robyn too, if one could judge by the trusting brown eyes she turned to him, and now, as he put his hand on her quarters to steady himself, she seemed to know that he was shaken with trouble, for her chain sawed as she turned her head and pressed against him, and her moist muzzle sought his hand.

Four of the horses were to go, the four best, and Starlight hadn't been told yet. If he were to tell her now it wouldn't be the same as telling a living soul, and she couldn't tell the others, for the Bible said that such as she were brute beasts without understanding. Moving further along the stall he approached Starlight's silky-haired ear.

John Skyrme did not set up for a clever man, but he was no duller-witted than most, and he was still holding up the lantern. Suddenly, as Robyn was whispering his secret, he raised his voice.

'Speak a bit louder,' he said, and drew nearer as Robyn began to unburden himself to the mare.

'At eight o'clock to-morrow night it's to be. Four of you's

to be at the yews in Hagthorpe Lane, and I'm to take you myself.'

For a moment the farmer seemed about to break out, but instead of doing so he followed Robyn further into the stall and dropped his voice. . . . 'Say that again,' he said.

'You're to have halters and your feed round your necks. It'll be corn. But if word could be got to Watty the kempery-man – I met him by the wall, going round telling 'em all – he was coming to Unthank, but he went round by the Point instead – so we'd best be ready — '

But at that John Skyrme no longer dropped his voice. The mare started as it broke harshly out.

'Then why the Sattan didn't you say so? Who do you say told you all this?' But Robyn, taking not the slightest notice, only went on talking to Starlight.

'And after I'd left the Stakes the Prince of Withernsea set on me. I couldn't see who they were, because they put a clout round my eyes, but he said it was his royal mother's orders, and fifteen of 'em were seen crossing from Holderness three days ago. We don't put our beasts out to gistment at Unthank, but those that do's got to get them in — '

John Skyrme needed no more enlightening. Robyn fell back before his wrathful oath.

'That cannibal crew again!' he roared. 'The Prince o' Withernsea and his royal mother! Stop that mumbling and speak out! The Prince o' Withernsea! Where was this, and how many of 'em, and where are they now?'

But seeing him so fierce Robyn was now more afraid than ever, and the last of the rum was working in his stomach again.

'Ugh – ugh — ' he reached.

'And my winter's store o' liquor gone, and you say Watty's out raising the cry! I was to blame for sending you that far alone, but how was I to know? The Prince o' Withernsea! Ay, and the King of Hell for that matter, for three of her sons she's bred up to be her tallymen! But by God, I'm King of Unthank as long as I'm here! To York on a hurdle's her royal coach if *I* can come nigh her!'

'Ugh – ugh — '

'Get you to the house and send Sim here. To-morrow night did you say? Tell Sim I want him! And creep you into bed before Margaret sees you! Four o' my horses! Send Sim here, quick — '

'I haven't told a living soul — '

'Come — ' and seizing the pitchfork, which Robyn still held, he thrust him out of the stable into the yard.

Robyn Skyrme himself had no hand in what took place the following evening, where Hagthorpe Lane ended at the yew trees and the undulations of the sandhills began. If Watty the kempery-man had been his father as like as not he would have 'blooded' him before things went any further, so making him more apt for whatever was to come. He would have made him one of the dozen men he posted at the likeliest points that night, have given him a whistle to blow when the moment came, or some other lad's part in the business to play. But John Skyrme did not cease to blame himself for having sent a boy on a man's errand. He ought to have had somebody with him, and while the horses remained peacefully in their stalls that night, it was by John's strict orders that Robyn, too, remained behind with the women, with a bandage round his aching neck and a bowl of gruel before him, almost as sick as before with the listening and the tension and the fear. He was in bed when the men returned, at some time after midnight, and even in the days that followed he was not told in one piece what had happened, but a bit at a time, in this version or that, leaving his imagination to fill in the rest.

This it did the more readily, that already he had the foundations to build on. A bandage had been bound over his own eyes, but it appeared that this time the marauders had blackened their faces, so that they should not be known or marked, and the encounter had been so short and sharp that they had not had time to carry their two wounded away. One of these, shot in the breast with John Skyrme's own brass blunderbuss crammed with nails and the rusty rivets of an old harrow, was the Prince of Withernsea himself, and he had died within the hour. The other, Robyn gathered, was still living, but nobody told Robyn where he had been carried, and it was nearly a week before one of the hinds let out what had happened even to the Prince's body. Then he learned that it had been shovelled into a hole down by the creek, and the tides had refused him and cast him up again, but the hungry sea-birds had not been so particular. By this time Robyn was out and at work again, but no longer the same Robyn. He was silent, whereas before he had been merry; nervous, whereas before he had been bold. He hardly went near Starlight, to feel whose springiness under him had hitherto been his joy. Somebody had told after having been warned not to tell. The Prince of Withernsea was dead, another not likely to live. And in her pocket the Prince's royal mother kept a stone, that after seven years she turned and spat on, but always threw in the end. This was the shadow under which young Robyn now had to live his life.

4

JOHN SKYRME could neither read nor write, but kept his accounts either in his long head or by certain private marks of his own on the chimney-breast of the long hall that served Unthank as a general living-room. But he had other plans for Robyn, and a number of years before had picked up as a sort of handyman an odd, vagabond sort of fellow who had taken Robyn's schooling in hand. He had worked for John for a couple of years before taking himself off again nobody knew where, and as Robyn had proved an apt scholar the farm accounts had now been turned over to him.

But it was up in his own belfry chamber that he kept his treasured six books, and when he had come to the end of his candles he read by rushlight. He was not the first to have done this, for the old Bible, as broad and thick as a door-step, resembled old church music, so close had the dead hands held the dip to the page, underscoring each line with its track of smoky brown. But it was downstairs in the hall that the accounts were gone into, with John at hand if anything had to be explained.

'Robyn lad,' said John one evening some three weeks after the affair of Hagthorpe Lane, 'get out my shoeing account. It's on my mind Dick Harding is shoeing half the horses in Lincolnshire at my expense,' and out the shoeing account had come, with that end of the long board cleared, for it was John's idea of writing that it needed plenty of elbow-room. As it was seldom that the whole establishment sat down at the same time, the other end of the board was set for the remaining suppers.

But as Robyn wrestled with the shoeing account he was aware of Margaret Skyrme as she passed in and out, preparing the next supper as she cleared away the last one, for Margaret, in setting her cap at Unthank, had had to take John Skyrme as she found him, not a widower, yet with a child about the place already beginning to walk. And in marrying her, John had made one condition. Whose child Robyn was was his business and nobody else's, and when John chose you might as well try to dig a secret out of the grave as get one out of him. Margaret was still handsome in her close-browed and forbidding way, but she herself was childless, and a by-blow afield all day was a by-blow out of sight, but not when he was as constantly about the house as if he had been afraid to set foot out of doors. She caught a few words of what her husband was saying as she passed with the platters.

'It's all over now, so put it out of your head, lad,' he was saying to Robyn in a subdued voice, very much as Robyn had muttered to Starlight. 'It was all a lot of blustery stuff meant to frighten you. A Prince? He's no more a Prince than I am. He's best dead, and the rest of 'em the same.'

But Robyn was answering in the same disquieted voice. 'If I couldn't see him because of the bandage, how did I know he was so big?'

'Big he was, there's no denying, as big as a door. You must have heard it somewhere. That's the way tales get about.'

'And didn't he squint?'

'Like Old Nick he did, but you've heard that too, and there's a thing I've been wondering. Do you think you're big enough to be trusted with a pistol if I was to give you one?'

And that was better, for at the mention of a pistol Robyn pricked up his ears – 'A real one?'

'To be sure. All the coach-guards carry pistols, and travellers, and I could soon put you in the way of using it.'

So half the next day Robyn spent in polishing up and cleaning a short half-pistol, squatting in the great hearth with a saucepan and the bullet-mould, casting lead bullets for it. On the broken door of an old shed John drew him the outline of a man to practise on, only warning him to let them know when he was going to shoot, so as not to startle Jessie at her milking or Mehitabel as she pegged out the washing or went out to gather the eggs. But even this did not please Margaret Skyrme, who spoke her mind to John when Robyn was out of the way.

'Why doesn't he take it away to the sandhills somewhere?' she scolded. 'Helping with the washing and carrying the pails! A month ago you never knew where to look for him, he was either with the fishermen down at the Stakes or setting snares or one thing or another! He's half as big again as young Giles, but last week when I told him to take Starlight and ride over to Mixton to get me a packet of needles he turned as white as camomile, and I had to take Giles off his work instead.'

'Give him time. He's a bit higher-strung than Giles. He had a turn that night, and he'll be better soon.'

'High-strung, him that can carry a sack of flour on his back! Helping with the dishes and making the beds! The wenches can do all that, and by the time he's finished bolting the doors at night you'd think the place was York Castle, all that iron and oak and bars and chains! I thought freckles meant the iron was in their blood!'

'Let be,' John ordered, in a tone that made her twitch her mouth but keep it closed, and her husband walked out of the hall.

But there was no keeping it from Robyn that they were at issue about him, and he began to spend many of his evenings, not with the rest of them, in the house, but with Sim Dacres, the head-hind, for Sim was married and had his own quarters adjoining the mistals across the yard. These consisted of the lower room and the overhead loft where Sim and Gillian slept, and as Gillian never let the peats on the hearth go out there was always something in the pot on the hook. The walls of the lower room were hardly to be seen for Sim's miscellany of belongings, his great-coat and muffler, the horse-pistol and powder-flask on their nail, his long skates, bundles of herbs, helves and handles set to season, his staff and heavy boots against the corner cupboard. He was for ever making or mending something, stitching a strap or filing at his bits of iron, and for all the years he had been at Unthank he was still a foreigner, for he came from the Bateable Land, where according to him the horse-stealers of Holderness might go to school to learn their business. But his dry expressions took the edge off some of the fearsome tales he told, not like the Book of Martyrs, that never left the nerve alone.

And there was Sim's daughter Polly, just Robyn's age, who coughed terribly but had silky chestnut hair, that she dried before the fire when she washed it and went on shaking out for the rest of the evening. Gillian said her cough would soon go when she got married, for she had her own ideas about Polly and her future, but Sim would glance up from his filing or whatever he was doing.

'Ay, we know about going to bed to save candles,' he would say in his humorous sour way. 'You wouldn't buy many candles for what *that* 'd save you by the end of the year!' he would chuckle, and Robyn would get ready to give Polly her spelling lesson.

But whatever Polly learned from the lessons, what Robyn was now quick to learn from them was a very different thing. Whoever cured Polly's cough by marrying her it wouldn't be Robyn, and yet he found himself thinking of Polly when he got upstairs to his own chamber again. It was the way her hair sometimes brushed against his cheek. It didn't excite or disturb him in any way, and yet somehow he felt as if some sea-wall had been breached, and for all her cough and hen-wittedness Polly helped to stop it again. Also it took his mind off Jessie Byers, who, as even Robyn could see, was the sort to make a bigger breach than she mended.

Under Margaret Skyrme Jessie had everything to do with the dairies, and John Skyrme, seeing her and her milking-stool at Umpleby Stattis, coming out of an inn with a couple of carter-lads with ribbons on their whips, had thought twice about having her in the house. But there had been a lack of milking-wenches just then, and in the end he had engaged her. Half her year was already up, and during most of that time Robyn hadn't taken any particular notice of her; but now he had begun to find himself looking at her when he thought she wasn't looking at him. Several times he had seen Dickon the cowman, passing her in the mistal or going into the dairy, pinch her or run his fingers up the nape of her neck and into her hair, and this nape, when she hung her head, seemed to split up into two white ropes above the knuckly bone a bit lower down. When she took her working-boots off of an evening in front of the hearth, moving her toes up and down inside her thick homespun stockings, he now couldn't help noticing how slim and small her feet were. When Polly Dacres shook her hair down there was no telling what shape her head was, but the head above Jessie's nape was as tight and round as a nut, and there always seemed to be space to spare between her and her clothes.

Until the affair of the Lane, it had been Robyn's habit to go upstairs early, so that he might read before he got into bed, or, if the night was cold, in the bed itself. But now he put off going, lingering downstairs for the sake of the company and the sound of the voices. Each had his separate occupation of an evening, Robyn his books or his accounts or perhaps carving something with his penknife, Mehitabel and the girl known only as Sally their spinning or mending, John Skyrme his ponderings for the morrow, and the hinds coming in one by one for their supper as they finished their work outside. And they were sitting so one evening when Robyn, humped in the settle corner nearest the hearth, suddenly got up. He felt restless, and might as well be in bed. He took his candle from the row on the dresser, lighted it at another candle, and with a grunted good night to everybody made for the door that led upstairs.

To get to his bedroom he had to take the long whitewashed upper passage, and then, at the handrailed stairs at the end of it, to ascend again. The passage itself continued to where the women slept, and only they and John Skyrme and Margaret and Robyn used that way at all, for the hinds had their own staircase, 'so', Sim Dacres said, 'that the women shouldn't get at 'em.' But that night Robyn had just reached the foot of his own stairs when he saw a light ahead. He had missed Jessie from downstairs and had supposed her to be in the back kitchen. Now through an open door a light shone, and as he watched a shadow crossed the light. It was Jessie, moving about as she went to bed.

But as Robyn was about to take his own turning he suddenly went hot-and-cold. She must have heard him or seen his light, for she stood in the doorway, fully dressed, with her own candle in her hand. She was not going to bed, but downstairs again, and she was standing the way she did stand, pressed flat as a leaf against the door-jamb, with her head a little down and the candle-light making two little beads of brightness in her dark eyes. She turned the eyes sideways on him.

'Good night,' she said in her small brook-like voice.

At that moment Robyn could not have given her her good night back, for suddenly he had a helpless, unprotected sort of feeling, as if everybody at Unthank knew far more about him than he knew himself. Polly Dacres knew it because of the things she did to her hair. Mehitabel and Sally knew it from the way they sometimes hemmed and stopped talking the moment they heard his foot. Margaret Skyrme knew it because not to like anybody is not to rest till you have found out the worst about them. And even John Skyrme said that Jessie was a slut and more trouble about the place than she was worth, but there she was, still not moving from the doorway of her room, though only the moment before she had started to go downstairs. She was only three or four strides away. He could almost smell the dairy on her, the buttermilk and curds and the salt of the butter, and it went to his head like the rum he had drunk seated on the cobbles at the end of the sea-wall. If she was a slut that smell, too, would make him sick afterwards, as the rum had made him sick, but at that moment she looked at him again, a couple of steps there up the stairs.

'Good night,' she said softly again, and all in a moment out went her candle. He heard her little start, as if it had gone out by accident. 'Oh, and now I haven't a light!'

Hardly knowing what he did, Robyn stooped and placed his own candle down where he was standing and fled up the stairs, his shadow making a monstrous blurr on the whitewash of the wall.

But such things are not to be got rid of by running away from them. His throat was tight and his heart thumping violently as he reached his own room and got out of his clothes and into bed, but even in bed his thoughts grew no calmer. The first of them to frighten him was his candlestick, which was a wooden one that he had carved himself, with an R.S. on it. With a shock it came over him that it might be found in Jessie's room. Even if she had placed it back on the lower stair after lighting her own at it, his father would see it and wonder what it was doing there – no, worse, for his father did not pass the foot of the stairs. The other girls would see it, and again he had that uncovered, unprotected feeling, as if to hide his thoughts away from the men was a simple thing, but the women peered and pried into them at their pleasure.

Then again he began to feel the new excitement coming alive in his breast. He needed no telling what Polly Dacre's bedroom was like, for while Sim and Gillian slept upstairs her bed was down below, because Gillian said it was good for her cough that she should sleep in a room that had been lived in during the day But he knew nothing of any other, and now he knew that there must be all the difference in the world between Jessie Byers's bedroom and Polly's. Jessie had a room to herself, because it was the smallest, Mehitabel and Sally sleeping in the next one, and girls had a different kind of clothes to take off, and brushes and pins and what not, and smaller shoes for when they walked out. He could see how small Jessie's feet were any evening when she took her great boots off, and suppose that instead of putting his candle down on the stair and then running away he had advanced those few paces, and like Dickon, run his fingers up her nape and into her hair? But the next moment he was wondering about the candlestick again. He hadn't heard her go downstairs, and perhaps by this time she was in bed, thinking of Robyn as he was thinking of her and feeling him in her blood the same way.

Then he heard the distant closing of the hall door and his father's step on the stairs. He hadn't heard Margaret, and John Skyrme was always the last up, and it was time Robyn went to sleep.

But sleep kept stubbornly away from him, and using one emotion to keep out another is all very well, but in opening the door we must be on the watch lest the enemy should slip in too. Young Robyn, lying there awake, now wondering what would have happened if he had advanced those few steps towards Jessie and the next moment listening for sounds, could not fail but hear them. It was a night without a moon, and the star-sprinkled sky made a dim shape of his window, and as a horse stamped in the stables he was suddenly thinking of Starlight. He dozed, and the next time he woke tried to think of Jessie, but somehow her magic was already stale and other thoughts thrust her image roughly aside. He was on the sea-wall again, with Watty the fenman bobbing up and down on his stilts like a goblin against the sky. He was blundering into the Stakes again and bruising his face, and after another interval was seated on the cobbles, unbuckling his pack and taking a swig of the rum because he had heard that liquor made a man feel brave. He had put his pack on again, and was making for the yew trees and Hagthorpe Lane, singing *Follow the Horses* at the top of his voice—

And by the time he had got to that point there were no longer any Jessies in the world, and it all came back to him by leaps and bounds. Suddenly he was being set on, blindfolded, hustled into the sandhills, harshly questioned. He felt the giant Prince's breath on his face again, the knife at his throat. He heard that other cruel voice saying, 'Tell him again, Prince, in case he forgets,' and again the knife-point, and the grim threat, that the Prince's royal mother never said things twice —

And now the Prince was dead, and what had happened to the other man he did not know, but all at once Ruff the yard-dog gave a low growl that turned Robyn's blood cold.

It was no good saying these things only happened to other people and a long way off. Everywhere there were footpads on the roads, gypsies who left their marks on walls and gate-posts. He did not hear Ruff growl a second time, but gypsies always had poisoned meat for dogs before they slit their throats. Shamed by his foster-mother, he had not bolted and chained the doors for several nights, there was no sound from Sim's quarters, but if Ruff was dead the house would be left unguarded. Suddenly with a bound Robyn was out of bed and at the door of his room.

A ladder led to the belfry and the house-bell. It creaked beneath Robyn's weight as he sprang barefoot up it, pushed at the trap at the top, and climbing out seized the rope that ran down through two floors to the outer porch. The bell shook out clang after clang into the night as Robyn grasped the rope and pulled.

But by the time John Skyrme had run up in his night-gown, with the rest of the household behind him and Sim Dacres calling as he ran across the yard, Robyn, who could carry a sack of flour on his back, was shivering with cold and wide awake again, looking down at them through the trap with a face as white as a camomile-flower.

5

THE most curious thing about the episode was the way in which it seemed to clear the air for everybody but Robyn, for there was not one of them but had his explanation of it. Margaret Skyrme, who had never held with all this reading, put it down to those six books Robyn had upstairs in his room. Gillian Dacres said that he must have done it in his sleep, as if to have done a thing in your sleep was almost the same thing as not having done it at all. Sim, her husband, cracked his joke about fetching people in to dinner in the middle of the night, and what Mehitabel and the rest said, Robyn, sullen and ashamed, could only guess at. But he knew that the one thing they agreed on was the one thing they did not say, and that was that instead of putting the past behind him he was brooding on it, and that for all the freckled iron in his blood it was his timorous and womanish nature peeping out.

Thus set apart, as if something in him that couldn't be helped had to be put up with, Robyn could not now go into the stables without fancying he saw reproach even in Starlight's brown eyes. He groomed her as before, but he never got on her back, and it was part of his isolation that if a distant errand was to do it was Dickon the cowman or one of the others who did it, while Robyn remained behind in the safety of the farm. The less his foster-mother said the more he knew she was thinking, and that it was only the fear of John Skyrme that kept her from putting it into words.

The weekly baking was done in the large back kitchen, and in a sense the kitchen always had been Robyn's job, that is to say, that if its chimney needed sweeping it was Robyn who got the brush and the rope, Robyn who fetched the water for its boiler, Robyn who lighted the fire in its large brick oven and raked the embers out again when the bread was ready to go in. And Margaret Skyrme had rolled up her sleeves one baking-day and was busy with her flouring and dredging when suddenly she spoke to Mehitabel.

'The afternoons are drawing in,' she said. 'We shall have Christmas on us before we know where we are. Then there'll be a pig to kill and the pork to salt, and nutmegs and allspice'll be to fetch from Mixton. That'll be a journey for Dickon.'

Robyn, busy at the oven, heard but said nothing, which did not mean that he thought nothing, for after many struggles he had made up his mind. The next time there was a distant errand to run he intended to take it upon himself, and there is no knowing but he might have come boldly out with his offer there and then, but at that moment the back window was darkened. A tall straggle-bearded figure was passing it with a pair of stilts over his shoulder, and the next moment Watty the fenman stood in the doorway, asking whether he might come in. Margaret, dusting the flour from her forearms, made him welcome, for it was not often his face was seen at Unthank, and he asked her whether the maister was anywhere about.

'He cannot be far away. Go seek him, Robyn,' said Margaret, and Watty turned to Robyn, whom he had not noticed.

'Good e'en to you, captain. The last time you and me met you gave me a hand with my stees over the wall. They tell me you had a bit of a shake-up after that,' and Margaret rapped sharply with her wedding-ring on the edge of the kneading-bowl.

'Robyn! Watty was speaking to you! Where are your manners?'

'Nay, it's the maister I came to have a word with,' said Watty, and Robyn went out to find him.

But so seldom was Watty's face seen at Unthank that already Robyn could give a guess as to what had brought him here to-day. He had come with news of some kind about the second man.

He had guessed rightly. For an hour that afternoon John Skyrme and the weatherbeaten old kempery-man had the large hall to themselves, while Robyn, carrying the loaves outside to cool and setting the kitchen to rights again, made feverish guesses at what kept them so long. Then his foster-mother came in again.

'You're to go in; they want you,' she said, and Robyn took off his apron and reached for his jacket.

The two men were seated together on the settle, and as Robyn entered he thought his father looked harassed and constrained, and that there was more than usual consideration in his voice.

'Here's my lad. Get a chair, Robyn,' and Robyn, too, drew up to the settle. 'You'd best tell him your own way,' and Watty rubbed his hands together and spoke briskly.

'Well, captain,' he said, 'I hear you've got a pistol now.'

Robyn waited.

'Well, the best of a pistol to my thinking's when there's no call for it, but it's a friend for all that. Things has come to a pass when honest folk has to go about armed.'

'They've come to a pass when thieves get so proud and lazy they don't do their own stealing, but send their orders as if they were kings and emperors,' John Skyrme growled, and Watty turned to Robyn again.

'But maybe you've heard the news?'

'No,' said Robyn in a low voice. 'Do you mean the other's dead too?' And again the fenman became brisk.

'Dead? Ay, but that isn't the news. Come to that he died a week ago, and if I'd had my way he'd ha' been buried like the other, where neither ebb nor flow would have him. This come of giving heathen Christian graves to sleep in.'

'Tell me,' said Robyn faintly.

'Some of 'em's been here again. They came the other night with a kelp-cart, and dug him up and took him away, quicklime and all.'

Had Robyn then truly heard something on that night when he had rung the bell? He managed to get out a 'When?'

'It might have been a Tuesday or it might have been a Wednesday. We didn't take much notice, nobody having been round that way.'

'But they went straight back, and nowt's been heard of 'em since,' John Skyrme put in hurriedly, for he had seen the look on Robyn's face.

'And they left a quittance lapped round a stone. I hear you can read?'

Robyn nodded, but Watty shook his head.

'Nay, I haven't got the paper. The justices has it, or the steward or the lord-lieutenant for all I know. If they'd made me adjutor, that was only a corporal, I'd ha' had a regiment out by now, not a few farmers with their hayforks. They're sharp enough at your door when their own taxes is to collect! Protection — ! But t'other lot, it seems they have a scholar among 'em. It's in Exodus twenty-one.'

'Go fetch the Bible,' John Skyrme ordered, and Robyn rose and went out.

But, smokily underscored by the old rushlights, Robyn had read what was in Exodus twenty-one before he left his chamber again. By the light that always remained a little longer at the top of the house he read:

'*And if any mischief follow then thou shalt give life for life, eye for eye, tooth for tooth, hand for hand, foot for foot —*'

He turned over the page and read on:

'*— burning for burning, wound for wound, stripe for stripe —*'

Slowly, with the Bible under his arm, he descended to the hall again.

The fenman stayed to an early supper, and Robyn too took his usual place above the hinds, but only at intervals did he raise his eyes to their guest across the board. He could not forbear wondering how many men the old soldier had slain with those same hands that now put the food into his mouth. It seemed impossible that he, Robyn, should ever live through what these grown grim men had seen and survived. And the hut in which Watty lived was many miles away, and he could have spent the night where he was if he had pleased instead of stalking off alone into the dark fens, but after supper he rose to go. The duck would be flighting early, he had his lines to lift and the round of his snares to make, and it was time he was on his way. But Sim Dacres had come in, and sat on after Watty had left, and the ball Watty had started Sim kept rolling. He would be sorry for any two who molested Watty on his way home, he said, for all the encumbrance of his stilts. Pistols made a noise, but the bolt from that crossbow of Watty's was home before you heard the twang, and even a brace of pistols was no more than two shots, and on he went till John Skyrme ordered him to stop.

And Mehitabel, gaping at Sim, was admiring him for the daredevil he must have been in his time, but Robyn's eyes were seeking the secret magic of Jessie again. This time she had taken her house-shoes off to warm her toes, and as Robyn glanced at his candlestick on the dresser he thought what a tale it could have told if it had had a tongue. If he had been ordered to saddle Starlight and ride to Mixton there and then it is likely he would have obeyed without a word, but he thought of Watty again, and was thankful he need not stir out of the house, for he had a feeling that in his rough way at least his father understood him. So he sat on and on till only his father and himself remained downstairs in the hall, but his father said no more about that afternoon's tidings, and without further speech they both went to bed.

As it happened, it was not Robyn but Margaret Skyrme who did not rest that night. It appeared that the feathers of her bed-ticking were beginning to work their way through again, and so badly did she sleep that she gave her orders the moment she set foot downstairs the next morning. The ticking must be resoaped, and the three girls must see to it before she laid herself in that bed again.

Because the soaping was a downy, sneezy business (for the great square bedding had first to be emptied and turned inside-out) it was a job best done outside, and a kitchen table had been dragged out and placed by the same barn door where John Skyrme had drawn the outline of the man for Robyn to practise his pistol-shooting. Mehitabel, Jessie and the girl who had no other name but Sally had pinned sheets about themselves and mobbled up their heads in kerchiefs to keep the flying particles out of their hair, and Jessie had tied her kerchief just over her brows, where the knot stuck out in two impudent little horns. They had shot the feathers out into a corner of the barn, and with their sleeves rolled up were all three busy at the soaping of the great striped bag, when Robyn happened to pass with a couple of buckets of meal. As he did so Jessie looked coaxingly up under her kerchief.

'Empty the bolster for us, Robyn,' she said, and Robyn put down his buckets and carried the unstitched bolster into the barn, where he shook out its feathers with the rest. When he returned they had finished the ticking, and again Jessie looked up.

'Give us a hand with the filling,' she said. 'Sally can finish the bolster, and we can hold while Mehitabel stuffs the feathers back,' and the three of them passed into the barn.

How much of it they had made up between them Robyn never knew, but before the ticking could be filled it had first to be turned the right side out again, and Robyn was head and shoulders in it, while Jessie also groped and fumbled to seize the bottom of it. This brought their heads almost into contact, and suddenly Robyn was startled as he had not been startled since that night by the yew trees that he was so desperately struggling to forget. Mehitabel, with a squeak of fun, had given the ticking a quick tug, pulling it down over the pair of them, and was dragging the striped stuff still further about their knees.

A stranger, more huddled place for a tryst could hardly have been found. No tiptoeing with candles in bedroom doorways now. Inside the bed itself, close in the soapy sheeting on which John Skryme and Margaret slept, Robyn heard Mehitabel's giggle outside.

'I've got my needle and thread – I'm sewing you both in!'

Jessie's nape was turned to Robyn, but he heard her treble voice and felt her breath as she struggled in their stuffy prison.

'You see if I don't serve you out for this!'

Then it seemed to him that she was no longer struggling, but waiting for Mehitabel to let them out.

And the Bible told Robyn that he must not give his strength unto women, but though only a little time before he had been reading how Rahab had hidden the men under the flax-stalks spread out on the roof his springtime and his pride were on him. As if it went there of itself, his hand was where Dickon's had been, running up her nape and into her kerchiefed hair, while she again struggled a little, but held her breath, as if she would have held it for ever and his own with it. In that strained pause of not-breathing she pressed the length of her body against him, clasping him so, till of a sudden he gripped her fiercely closer and pushed her violently away again, as if in one movement. She too, snatched at the ticking, which Mehitabel was no longer holding. She got it clear of their heads, and as she did so a handful of goose feathers in their faces caused them both to choke and splutter. Spitting the down from his mouth, and with a second handful of feathers powdering the air behind him, Robyn broke for the house.

6

HE had a feeling of irreparable sin. It could only be the sin the scriptures meant when they said it pierced the liver like a dart and poured out the bowels like water, and he trembled to think of its punishment. His handful of books were in a recess of his garret wall, all but the Bible, which was too big for it and had to lie flat on the table, and he glanced fearfully up at the Book of Martyrs. Often and often he had been afraid to open that terrible book because of its pictures, and even now there were certain pages he hurried over three or four at a time, but to-day it was not the joyous deliverance but the martyrdom itself that seemed to speak with a voice of thunder. It might be that these devoted ones had lighted a candle in England that should never be put out, but must – oh, must that recanting right hand be the first to be thrust into the flames? And the Register was even worse than the Book of Martyrs, for the hammer-like repetition of its interminable list of names tolled in the affrighted ear like passing-bells. And yet the world seemed to go on just the same, with Dickon, whom he heard down below, softly whistling through his teeth at his work, as if he too did not lie under the same damnation! It could only be that Robyn was in some way different, and as he got down on his knees and tried to pray, but couldn't for trembling, this difference haunted him again.

For, sometimes coming and sometimes going, it had always haunted him, that day when his father would take him out into the fields, where there was nobody to hear, and begin 'Robyn lad, you're getting a young man now, and there's something it's on my mind to tell you,' and on that day his father would tell him what not even Margaret Skyrme knew – who his mother was. He had assumed she was dead, though John Skyrme had never said so, so how if, when that day came, John went even further, and told him to get into his best kerseys and neckcloth and shoes, and pack his bundle, for there were reasons why his mother could not come to Unthank, so he was to be taken to see her, perhaps not to return? That, at any rate, would be the last of Hagthorpe Lane and the Prince of Withernsea and the dead man whose body had been dug up again and carried away in a kelp-cart.

So Robyn tried to say his prayers but couldn't because of other things, and downstairs he went again, and out of the house by the back way, avoiding everybody in his desire to suffer alone where none could see him.

But the jest had got abroad, for as he passed Sim's cottage the head-hind called to him from his doorway.

'It's flocks and straw for us, Robyn, but what's this about the maister and mistress sleeping on feathers?' And, as Robyn made no reply, he chuckled. 'Well, dirty water's good enough to quench a fire with,' but by that time Robyn was out of earshot.

It was on a Friday that Robyn had been trapped in the bedtick with Jessie Byers, and he spent the Saturday up in the eight-acres, building a turnip-clamp and going in to his supper before the rest so as to get upstairs to his own room. But on the Sunday morning he was downstairs before anybody but the girl called Sally was out of bed, and Sally's eyes grew big at the sight of Robyn, in his best-ribbed kerseys, his homespun grey stockings and holiday shoes, with his best neckerchief round his neck.

'Whatever can be to do, Robyn?' she asked, for when she had filled the kettle and got the fire going she, too, intended to creep back into bed for another half hour.

'Cut me some bread and meat. Then you can tell them I've gone to Mixton,' Robyn replied.

'What to do at Mixton, on a Sunday?' she asked, for except when somebody was to marry or bury or a child to christen, out-of-the-way places like Unthank troubled Mixton and its church little.

'You get on with your own business,' said Robyn, and went out to saddle Starlight.

Unthank belonged as much to the shore as it did to the inland parts, and it was now nearly two months since he had last been beyond its confines. Indeed, the eight-acres of the turnips was almost the farthest he had ventured, and he had almost forgotten the brown stubble and the ploughing where the land began to rise, the crows' nests in the bare elms and the overarching vastness of the sky. He had almost forgotten, too, what it all looked like from Starlight's back, and as he closed the last of the Unthank gates behind him his blue eyes lighted up at the sight of the thorn bushes scattered over the fields because of the men who came with their nets by night. There might be perils ahead, but there were perils at home too, to have chosen a church as his destination somehow turned what else would have been a venture into a pilgrimage, and with his pistol in his pocket and Starlight between his knees he felt as if he was leaving a blackness and a cloud behind him.

Besides, with Christmas over, it would soon be spring. He could do most things about a farm, Umpleby Stattis was in February, or, for that matter, there was a good deal to be said for going to sea, to Antwerp in Roger's hoy perhaps. He didn't suppose that the sea hadn't its perils too, of privateers and herring-sploshers and Dutchmen who thought the seas belonged to them, but it would be like starting with a clean sheet and no old scores to settle, and he was thinking of Roger and his hoy when a pheasant whirred almost under Starlight's feet. It streamed away, and as he watched it out of sight his eyes wandered further still. Hardly a chimney smoked yet, he and Starlight had the world to themselves. There had been no floods, and looking seaward he could see its rippling silver thread, the intersecting lines of the long dikes, a few lazy gulls and the twinkling black-and-white of the sheldrake as they rose and settled again. Looking the other way he could see Mixton village on its distant skyline, for the packroad crossed the shoulder of the hill, visible miles before you came to it, and the tall spire of its church served Roger for a landmark. They seemed to be repairing its roof, for the faint airy scaffolding about one end of it looked like the cobwebs on the hedges, beaded with their fairy mist.

But at the sight of the church Robyn reddened more than with the morning air. Though he knew his catechism he had never been confirmed, and if he ever came to be confirmed he would have to say that he had kept his body in temperance and soberness and chastity, whereupon he would be told that he was able to do none of these things of himself. He shook Starlight up to a canter for a quarter of a mile, and then dropped to a jog-trot again along the hedged and tree-grown lanes.

It was early afternoon, and the bells were ringing, as he made his way up Mixton's empty and Sunday-shuttered street and stopped at the inn next to the church. He saw to Starlight's feed and watering, and then, taking the short cut into the churchyard, walked round to the scaffolded side door, for the great one was closed. Mixton was a sizeable village, with shops and a weekly market, but he did not know why it needed so large a church, for there were not more than a handful of worshippers in its great grey emptiness as he tiptoed half-way up its length and slipped into a pew behind everybody else. High over his head the treble fluting of an organ seemed to be running round and round after its own echoes, but Robyn, not raising his eyes, could not tell where the sound came from. At any rate, it ought to be easier to pray in so great and cool and lofty a place than in his belfry-chamber at home.

But he began to glance about through his fingers instead. Quite close to him, sleeping on a flat stone table against the outer wall, a marble knight and lady lay side by side, and they seemed to find no difficulty in praying, for their palms were pressed flat together and their stone eyes were piously closed. The knight was in armour, with his feet crossed and his head on a plump bolster, but the lady's head was on a small square cushion with carved tassels, she had a sort of garter on one arm, and the flutings of her clothes ran in stiff straight lines from her wimple to her pointed feet, which were not crossed. Other figures lay on tables beyond them, and on the wall above was a large coat-of-arms in a heavy black frame, tilted up on one corner instead of being hung straight. But as Robyn presently began to peer about more boldly it was on the large amber window ahead that his eyes rested. Lying down at the foot of it, either dead or asleep with his cheek on his hand, the image of a man was painted on the glass, and out of his recumbent body sprang a tree. It grew straight up the middle of the window, with branches to right and left, and perched in the branches were little men or saints with vestments and mitres on their heads, sprinkling the window like little Christmas-candles. And at the top of the tree, letting through the light, hung the radiant figure of Jesus Christ in His glory, and looking at this Robyn was not quite sure when the music in the roof ceased and a solemn warning voice was raised instead.

'*When the wicked man turneth away from his wickedness —*'

In the same raised way the voice went on till it came to '*Saying after me*,' and then with the sound pebbles make on a beach when the wave has broken the voices of the congregation were raised too.

'Almighty and most merciful Father —'

And though the curate of the place had begun the next verse before the last of the trailing voices had caught him up, and Robyn knew that nothing in the world was more important than what they were all confessing and what he had come to confess too, still his eyes were wandering from object to object between his fingers. The stall-ends were of oak, finishing off with carved poppy-heads, and all were of different patterns – angels, animals, leaves, fruits, little men with crosses and books. The stone table on which the knight and lady lay was as artfully chiselled as the tassels of the lady's pillow and the garter on her arm. Its lower part was divided into narrow upright panels, and while half the little effigies of its niches had been knocked away the niches and slender foliage remained like empty frames, and Robyn himself knew how to carve the ears of corn on the bread platters and the R.S. on his wooden candlestick. If only he had had one of the effigies to copy from he could have cleared one end of the hall table, and sharpened his penknife and got a piece of seasoned wood, and in and out among the foliage he would have had little living things peeping and playing, field-mice and frogs and squirrels with their nuts and other harmless creatures.

And though he noticed that the people in front of him were kneeling, and knelt himself, and rose again when they rose, he did not join in the psalm because he was beginning to get shy of his altering voice. So he watched the stall-ends and the figures on the window instead, and knew very little more till in quite another voice he heard the words, 'Here beginneth the nineteenth chapter of the book of Isaiah.'

At first he didn't know what the words reminded him of. But as they began to piece themselves together before tailing off into their echoes again, he gathered that they were all about some day of reckoning to come, when every man should be fighting against his neighbour and a fierce king should rule over them all. And the air of the church was stagnant and cold, but Robyn felt a slow chill creeping into his blood too. Watty the kempery-man had come to Unthank that afternoon with a message from Exodus twenty-one that none of them could read. His father had sent him upstairs, and there in the great Bible he had read those menacing words about burning for burning and stripe for stripe. Even in Mixton church he could not get away from it, for the congregation sat very still as the quiet monotonous voice penetrated to every corner of the place.

'*The fishers also shall mourn, and all they that cast angle into the brooks shall lament, and they that spread nets upon the waters shall languish*—' the voice read, and Robyn forgot the knight and the lady and the broken figures in the niches as it went on:

'*And they shall be broken in the purposes thereof, all that make sluices and ponds for fish* — '

It seemed to Robyn that that meant the fishermen plying their trade at the Stakes and the men of the farms who turned out with every horse and cart and barrow when the sea-wall broke —

'*They have caused Egypt to err as a drunken man staggereth in his vomit* — '

That was how Robyn had staggered when he had drunk the rum, and fierce hands had been laid on him, and he had stumbled home to the stable to pour it all out into Starlight's ear —

'*In that day shall Egypt be like unto women, it shall be afraid and fear* — '

Then the book must have closed, for the voice ceased, and the 'Here endeth' was lost as a tremor ran through the church and the organ spoke again. Treble voices such as Robyn's had lately been rose in the *Te Deum*, and it was as the congregation joined in that Robyn, chancing to turn, saw the man four pews behind him.

Like Robyn, he was sitting in the corner of the pew nearest to the wall, and Robyn had no idea how long he had been there. And it was seemly that Robyn, a stranger to the place, should seat himself modestly behind everybody else, and this man, too, had the look of a stranger, for he was heavily coated, had clapped a broad hat over the poppy-head of the stall-end, and an immense staff he had placed on the ground projected from the end of the pew and half-way across the aisle. He was broad and brawny, and Robyn wondered why he had not left his staff in the porch, though for that matter he too had a pistol in his pocket. But the man lifted a single eye, for the other was a slit, and Robyn quickly dropped his own eyes again.

The feeling that he was being watched lasted till the end of the service. The congregation rose to sing, and the one-eyed man seemed to know the hymn too, but Robyn had good reason for knowing that it was not only the godly who were familiar with hymns and texts, and when he glanced round again he was perturbed to see the fellow and his staff just disappearing into the porch. Those of the congregation first to leave began to file past him. Stooping for his hat, which was under the seat, he joined the stream, and issuing from the porch slipped round by the scaffolding and stood half-hidden behind a buttress.

Then he saw why the man had carried his staff into the church. The people, instead of departing, were lingering, and outside the porch stood a closed chair. He saw not one man with a staff, but two, fitting them into the staples, and Robyn suddenly wanted to laugh, so was the weight lifted from his mind. Even at a church porch it was their habit to remove the staves from the chairs because of rogues and pilferers, the fellows were doubtless as honest as anybody else, and the chair must be waiting for some person of quality whom Robyn had not seen in the church. Stepping out from the concealment of his buttress Robyn, too, waited for this person of consequence to come out.

Suddenly there was a curtseying and a doffing of hats. The one-eyed porter was holding the chair door open, and from the porch into the chair there stepped a child of eleven, in a flowered brown paduasoy mantua that reached down to her toes, a close-fitting coif of gold mesh, and ringlets as gold escaping like little catkins down her cheeks. Her hands were in a muff, but she drew one of them out to help herself into the chair. A little ivory-backed psalter remained for a moment peeping out of the muff, and in its little green laced-up glove it seemed to Robyn that the hand on the edge of the chair was like the sheath in which opening lords-and-ladies were wrapped. The chair door closed, the two men took up their light burden, and Robyn watched it through the open lych-gate and out of sight.

7

SIM DACRES, forever making or mending something, had saws and chisels of sorts, and there was always plenty of wood set by to season for gates or shelves or repairs about the house, but Robyn's penknife was no longer enough for him and he wanted tools of his own. He had little use for money, and in the ordinary way possessed none, but if he wanted anything asked for it, and if it was anything in reason usually got it. The nearest place for such things as he now wanted was Umpleby, and in the ordinary way a journey to Umpleby and back meant two nights from home. It therefore filled Robyn with hope that, when he told his father that he wanted such and such tools, John Skyrme put his hand under his hat and scratched his head.

'Wait a minute till I bethink me,' he said. 'For carving wood did you say?'

'Yes,' said Robyn.

'There was an old clockmaker used to come here when you were no higher than my knee that I bought a lot of stuff of. It's somewhere in a kist upstairs. Leave it for to-night and we'll go up in the morning and have a look.'

And sure enough John, careful man, turned out from the old chest handful after handful of wooden clock-wheels and pulleys and leaden weights and hardwood pinions, like those of the clock in the hall downstairs, that worked with cords and wood and had only one hand. Stored away under all this litter were half a dozen tools Robyn now had a use for, and to work he set.

Woe betide any of the hinds who set as much as a finger on a tool once Robyn had got it sharpened to his liking. He cleared up his own litter after him, carried his pieces of wood back to his belfry chamber, and brought them down nightly again whenever there were no accounts to do. And as he sat there at his cleared end of the table, sawing and gouging and paring and frowning over his work, the night when he had rung the house-bell in his panic was forgotten, for if anything was to fetch from Mixton now there was Robyn, ready at a word to fetch it. On weekdays Mixton's shops and church were open alike, and when he had finished with Margaret Skyrme's nutmegs and allspice he usually turned into the church for half an hour, to see the knight and his dame lying on their double stone table and to make notes on his pieces of paper of the effigies in their niches below.

But though he asked at the inn who the young mistress was he had seen getting into the chair, and described her in her brown mantua and coif of gold thread, he could get no better answer than that she must have been visiting at one of the gentry's houses thereabouts and gone away again, and he had become afraid to ask further. Twice since then he had been to Mixton on a Sunday, but he had not seen her in the church again, and already the bright little picture she had made in his mind was beginning to fade. Christmas was close at hand, the countryside was quiet, and come Umpleby Stattis there would be no more Jessie Byers either, for John Skyrme was resolved not to have her under his roof for another year.

To Robyn it was as if she had already gone, for it is the magic that makes all the difference and somehow all the magic had gone from Jessie now. A magic he couldn't have described had taken its place, that had nothing to do with violent moments inside bed-tickings that left him as red and slack as a wattle, or with that disturbing space there always seemed to be between Jessie and her clothes. Jessie wore her garters on her slender legs, but the new magic was that of the lady lying by her knight on the tomb, who wore a single garter on her arm and did not seem to have any legs, so chastely did the undeviating lines of her draperies run down to her pointed toes. It belonged to the amber window with the little holy men sprinkled over it and the tree that grew out of the dead man at the bottom, and Jessie might now show that channel of her nape or take her boots off before the fire as much as she liked, but she kindled no flame in Robyn. One night, when his gouge slipped and ran deeply into his thumb, so that he could not use that hand again properly till Christmas Eve, it was Jessie who drew the gap together for him and put plaster on it and a bandage, yet her touch and the way she lifted her eyes excited him not at all.

But there was nothing holy about the air at Unthank, as there was at Mixton church, and it was hardly to be expected that poor Jessie's teat-hardened palms should have little green lord-and-lady gloves on them, like the child he had seen getting into her chair.

It had been a plentiful autumn for berries, and Unthank

always made up in berries and green leaves and extra cooking for its lack of church-going during the rest of the year. So that Christmas Mehitabel and Sally stuck the holly-sprigs everywhere, along the great overmantel, on the top of the one-handed clock, among the jugs and pewter of the dresser and on every cupboard top. Nobody said anything to Robyn about feathers when the two geese were plucked, and the iron door of the oven in the back kitchen clanged incessantly as Margaret Skyrme put in this or took that out. John Skyrme had come to some arrangement with Roger or his agent, for the lost medicines had been made good, and the outside work on the farm was well forward, so that there should be no need to get out of bed too early on Christmas morning. But as the day broke, and before the household was well awake, there was a loud knocking at the still closed front door, and Sim Dacres, who had been the cause of it, stepped back out of the porch and called up under John Skyrme's bedroom window.

'Maister! You'd best come down,' he shouted, and John Skyrme, getting hurriedly into his jacket and breeches, descended and unfastened the door. Out in the yard Sim pointed. Smoke was rising from beyond the steadings, and even at that distance there was an acrid smell in the air.

'It's the ricks,' said Sim, and a moment later John Skyrme had seized the bell-rope in the porch and was swinging away at the bell that had not been rung since the night when Robyn had brought the household out of bed by ringing it in his sleep. Ten minutes later every hind and woman in Unthank was racing for the steadings.

It was a dismal sight for a Christmas morning. There were half a dozen of the ricks, five of them new hay, and they were spaced well apart and there had been no wind out of the ordinary, yet already one of them could hardly be approached for the curds of choking smoke it emitted, and the rest of them were seeping and reeking as if they had been stacked wet. That all should have caught together put accident out of the question, and John Skyrme raised his voice.

'To it everybody – get hooks and forks – you women get to the pump with buckets and make a chain — '

The men made a rush to the outbuildings, Margaret Skyrme, with her nightgown showing under her petticoats, placed herself at the pump in the yard. The others, with their bare feet thrust into their heavy boots, ran hither and there with buckets. The men attacked the ricks with their forks, flinging hooked ropes over them to bring them down, but they were too late, for Robyn, driving a fork deep into a stack, started back as it showed an interior as red as a furnace, that at the entry of the air roared into fierce flame.

'Let that one be – turn to the far two!' John Skyrme choked, for he, too, had got a bellyful of the smoke, and to the farther two they turned, drenching them with water and seeking to clear the burning space between. But at that moment a light break-of-day wind sprang up, and there was a doubling of the roaring and of the grey and ashy-pink that rolled away in volumes towards the house. The heat on that side was insupportable, and their flushed faces were grimy with the ash and running sweat. It was barely possible to save more than half of the old and already settled stack, and by ten o'clock, beaten and exhausted, they had given it up. Dismally they stood looking at one another.

But not one of them said what each had in his mind.

Christmas dinner that day was hours late. It was six o'clock and night had long since fallen, before they settled themselves at the long board, with two small tables set across one end of it, for it was one of the days when they all sat down together, and Sim Dacres, Gillian and Polly also assisted at the melancholy feast. Outside the darkness was still broken by the glow that rose and fell again beyond the outbuildings, but the harm was done, the two stubble geese and the ribs of pork were not to be wasted, and the clatter of eating was no less that the best part of the winter's keep had gone. After the meats came the mincemeat and the great spiced loaf and cheese, and as a sign that other troubles might keep till the morrow John Skyrme got the spirits out. While Margaret Skyrme cut the loaf, Robyn went round filling the horns and pewter and earthenware, and when they had finished the women turned to clear away.

They had had fire and to spare that day, but none the less the Christmas logs were set on end to burn their merriest. With the board pushed back they drew up their seats in a great ring that stretched from the settle to the clock, and sat with the firelight on their faces and the flames in their thoughtful eyes. Robyn did no wood-carving that night, but listened to Sim Dacres instead, sitting next to Sally under the clock, for the spirits had set Sim off, and he took most of the conversation on himself. Even so, it flagged ominously, and it was into one of its pauses that Sim dropped one of his clipped and saturnine remarks.

'I warrant,' he said slowly, his eyes travelling round the ring, 'not one of you here knows what a hangman's wages is.'

'What a what is?' said Dickon, who always egged Sim on, and Mehitabel and Jessie nudged one another.

'I warrant,' said Sim again, 'nobody here knows what a hangman's wages is. What he gets for hanging 'em,' and as one by one they shook their heads, for none of them knew what the hangman got, he told them. 'They're thirteen-pence-ha'penny,' he said. 'That's what a hangman gets, thirteen-pence-ha'penny,' and Margaret Skyrme scolded him for bringing forward such a subject.

'Offald talk like that at Christmas! You're old enough to know better!' she rebuked him, but he only grinned.

'I thought Christmas night was the time,' he said.

'Then think again, something a bit more seasonable,' but Sim's eyes were travelling round the circle again.

'Nay, I was only counting,' he said. 'How many do you make us sitting here?'

Instantly other eyes too were counting, and Margaret came out with a sharp 'Have done!' In the ordinary way they would have been twelve, the three of the family, Sim's own three, the three hinds and the girls in the house. But two days before Harding, the farrier and shoesmith, who was a relative of Dickon's, had called and left behind him over Christmas a small urchin who slept in Dickon's bed and had taken up so little room at the board that they had hardly noticed he was there. Now he was the odd ha'penny, and at that moment Robyn, thinking he heard a sound in the yard, half rose from the settle, whereupon Sim spoke again.

'I should let somebody else get up first if I was you, Robyn,' he said.'They say that's the one it always happens to.'

But Robyn, almost certain that he had heard something, had already crossed to the door.

It had not been fastened, for half a dozen times one or other of them had looked out to see how the fire was dying down. He stepped out, but there was nobody in the porch, and drawing the door to behind him he took a few paces into the yard. From somewhere beyond Sim's quarters he heard the sound of men's voices. He had no light, but neither by day nor night was he without his pistol now, and as he advanced he heard the short sound of a horse shaking its harness. Peering cautiously round the corner past Sim's door he saw moving shadows, cast by the light of a lantern placed on the ground, and for all his care he must have heard, for a voice was raised.

'Is that the goodman?'

'No, that's my father. What is it?' said Robyn.

'Go fetch him,' and Robyn sped back to the house.

So it came about that what no Unthank tongue had uttered that day, though it had been in every breast, was there to speak for itself. Coming and going along the roads, seldom to be seen in any one place more than twice or so in the year, Old Nicholas the pedlar had been a figure of the countryside for as long as Robyn could remember. So well known were he and his pack that even alone he went unmolested, and when he appeared with his buttons and laces and combs for the hair and penknives for the pocket he was the carrier of distant news too, for he travelled beyond York to the north, returning by the Wolds or the Hornsea and Withernsea flats, crossing by Kingston-upon-Hull if there was a hoy or by the ferry at North Cave, and so south as far as Lincoln itself. Just a harmless old man, probably on his way to Unthank to taste their fare, and wish them a merry Christmas and perhaps do a bit of trade, and then sleep with his head on his pack before their fire —

But between York and Lincoln there was no place he would have done better to keep away from that day. The two mounted sheriff's men had found him like that on Unthank land, not far from the steadings, and Robyn, who had returned with his father, was looking at him as he lay there under Sim's wall with his throat cut. And quick as they were to drop a cloak over the rest, Robyn saw that too. Only fiends from the Pit could have devised and executed such a butchery on one whom a hundred times before they had let go free. Their vengeance was not on him, but on the ground he trod, its ricks and blunderbusses loaded with old harrow rivets, its cattle and all that dwelt under its roof.

But they had come upon old Nicholas and his pack instead, not a hundred yards from where the ricks still smouldered. Already Sim had appeared on the scene. A hurdle was brought and on it Nicholas was laid. They carried him to the same barn where the feathers had been emptied from the bed-ticking, and closed the bullet-pitted door with Robyn's outline of a man on it. Then one of the sheriff's men turned to John Skyrme.

'Goodman, you have your bed to go to to-night, and there's two of us here wishes we had the same. But we've Umpleby to make before this time to-morrow, for there's to be no sanctuary for this. It'll be hue-and-cry by proclamation, hutesium-and-clamor, with horns and shouts wherever they're seen, and them that doesn't help constable or sergeant'll smart for it. Leave that body where it is till the Umpleby coroner comes, and see it isn't touched. Them barbarians in Yorkshire can do as they like, but this is Lincolnshire. I see you've had a mishap to your ricks. Be thankful it isn't your house, and you'd best lay an information now while we're here. You can put it down person or persons unknown. The justices is taking a hand now.'

And when Watty the fenman heard of it he said it was high time.

8

WITH so little else of note in their lives, and so few to set down the little there is, the ruffians of the time are more likely to be remembered because their last bowl of ale was drunk in a tumbril or their last speech made with a rope round their necks than for any other difference they made in the world; yet it is not upon record that the justices of the region did anything in particular about whatever informations the folk of the region laid before them. If any militia turned out in force it would be to Holland or Ireland that they went, and not to the Unthank sandhills or the yew trees in Hagthorpe Lane. Again that winter the sea-wall was breached, making a second sea inland, a-swirl with tossing branches and the debris of stacks and the swollen bellies of beasts. There were those who came forward with evidence that an outlawed hand had made the hole. To go into that, however, would apparently have led to other trouble, and it was more edifying to proclaim it an Act of God.

But less easily forgotten than the inundations was the hard and protracted frost that followed them, and Robyn Skyrme, going into Sim Dacres' cottage one evening, found him as ever, busy with something. This time he had got down his long runner skates and was putting an edge on them with a sandstone strickle. And as he worked he hummed intermittently, half aloud and half to himself:

> '*For man, that's born of a middleyeard wight*
> *For wealth or pelf can ne'er be secure —*

'– haven't you finished brushing that hair yet, Polly? —

> '*For he may have enough owernight*
> *Yet in the morning wake full poor.*'

He looked up as Robyn entered.

'For the love o' God shut that door before it freezes the peats on the hearth!' he said. 'Hark to Polly's hair, crackling like crickets! They say it's five inches thick on Pelton Broad, and if it'll bear at Pelton it'll bear anywhere,' and he ran his thumb along the skate edge and squinted at it in the candlelight.

Robyn had altered. His birthday had been on the second of January, he had entered his fifteenth year, and his voice had found itself. His blue eyes looked straight at you, but with little alteration of expression, and they had an odd look of pausing in them, as if he had heard very well what you said but was waiting for the next to come. He had crossed the yard to Sim's that evening to have his hair cut, for Gillian did the cutting for the whole household, and on Sundays shaved Sim too, to begin his week's stubble anew. So between Polly's hair crackling like crickets as she brushed it on the edge of her bed, and Gillian's getting out the sheet to tuck into Robyn's neck, there was no need for Sim to sing, for he had plenty to comment on without.

'You'll be able to skate to church next Sunday barring a break comes,' he said, for the ironbound waters stretched almost to Mixton on its hill. 'You can tell the lanes by the hedge-tops sticking out. What the birds find to live on beats me. It's Polly has the warmest chamber to-night,' and he got up to push the mat closer under the door.

But as Robyn sat before the fire with the sheet over his shoulders, and Gillian started on his nape, he was not thinking of Polly and her frost-brittle hair. Sim had set his thoughts loose, and while Gillian snipped he was thinking of that first Sunday morning when he had ridden to Mixton church on Starlight, and after the service had seen two porters setting their staves into a chair, and into the chair had stepped a child of eleven, looking not less but more childish for the psalter in her muff and her grown-up mantua hardly showing her toes. Back at Unthank he had tried evening after evening to draw her like that, crumpling up his bits of paper afterwards and cramming them into his pocket and always ready to cover them up with his elbow if Margaret Skyrme or any of them passed behind him, because what they would have thought would have been a thousand miles away from the truth. A child like that! Why, not so long ago that hand in its little green glove had been holding a rattle or a coral with bells on it, whereas Robyn himself was now a great fellow who with a good grip on Sim's hand could have thrown the head-hind over his back. No, Robyn was not thinking of anything so foolish as that. He was thinking instead of the saint-sprinkled window, and of the knight and lady side by side on their table, and how it was that nobody at Unthank ever thought of going to church.

Naturally they couldn't all have gone. There was the dinner-cooking and the animals, and it was shaving-day for the men, and everybody had the odds and ends to do that they hadn't been able to find time for during the week. But Robyn had heard speak of houses, not great houses, but houses no bigger than Unthank, where the master himself took the parson's place, with the others kneeling as he read and prayed. It seemed to Robyn that in a world so uncertain as this people ought to be prepared for anything that might happen, as he was trying to prepare himself. There was the great rushlight Bible, and if his father couldn't read it he could, and as Gillian snipped and Sim rasped up his skate and Polly continued to brush out her hair he was wondering what his father would say if he were to speak of it.

'Get the razor and give him a lathering while you're about it,' Sim jested to Gillian. 'It's going to be ginger, Robyn – ginger for game they say — '

To see better what she was doing, Gillian had lighted a second candle, but even then Robyn had to turn on his stool from time to time as if he had been roasting before the fire on a spit. It so happened that one of these turns brought him facing the outer wall where Sim's greatcoat and other paraphernalia hung, and whether it was the basin or his head or the snip-snip of the scissors in his ears, off roamed his thoughts again. They went back to that Christmas night when they all sat together round the fire, trying not to think of the ricks though the smell of them was still in their nostrils. Then Sim had started that unlucky counting, and even before he had finished Robyn had thought he heard a sound in the yard, and had gone out to see what it was, and now he shivered again in spite of the heat of the fire. That was why he now looked long and doubtfully at people, as if he wondered what they were thinking of him. His eyes were on Sim's greatcoat on the wall, but only a couple of feet beyond it he could still see what he had seen that night by the light of the lantern on the ground – the horses of the sheriff's men, old Nicholas lying there with his throat cut, and the haste they had made to cover the rest up before he could see it. He had hoped to wear it down by frequent repetition, but there were times when it started up as fresh as ever, and always there were those fearful words of Exodus, as grue as thunder behind. As for the ricks, the sheriff's man had said it might as well have been the house itself with everybody sleeping in it, for set oil and turpentine to that timber framing and Unthank would have been Smithfield itself, and suddenly he winced and started, so that Gillian had to tell him to keep still, for the point of her scissors had pricked him under the ear.

So he sat still, but what was the use of thinking of Sunday prayers for Unthank with Umpleby Stattis now less than a month away? It was too late now to tell himself that it had been John Skyrme who had fired the blunderbuss that had laid the Prince of Withernsea low, Watty the fenman who had shovelled the Earl of Hornsea into that grave from which he had been dug up and carried away in a kelp-cart. It was he himself who had brought the trouble on them all, even on poor old Nicholas, for on any land but Unthank land he would surely have been allowed to go. So it was now best that Robyn himself should go. If in some way it could spread about that he was no longer there it might draw the trouble off again, and again he heard the head-hind's voice, talking out of the corner of his mouth to his wife.

'I wonder who the maister'll get in place of Dickon,' he suddenly said, and Gillian stood with her scissors poised in the air.

'In place of Dickon! Why should he want anybody in the place of Dickon?'

'Dickon's off come Umpleby, he says. As for that trollop Jessie, it beats me she didn't break her hiring at the six months when she had the chance.'

'Dickon off! Does he say what for?' Gillian exclaimed, and Sim reached for the other skate.

'He says three times in three months is enough for him and he isn't stopping for a fourth,' Sim replied cheerfully, and in the silence that fell Polly's hair could be heard crackling all by itself.

It was true. Hagthorpe Lane, the ricks, and old Nicholas the very same night: the rest of them might stay if they liked, but Dickon was going, and Gillian could only snap.

'Well, the pair of them's no great loss, and that Mehitabel wouldn't be either, for it's every morning in the week she calls downstairs she's just coming when she's still in her shift in bed.'

But as the silence continued Robyn was now occupied by a new thought. This was, that if Dickon and Jessie left, and himself at the same time, it would be thought that three times in three months was getting too often for him too.

The long hall table at Unthank might now have had a thundercloud for its ceiling instead of the good underdrawn flooring of the bedrooms overhead. John Skyrme's hirelings commonly stayed on with him year after year, for his wages were good and he treated them well. He would shed few tears over Jessie Byers, but another year would have been Dickon's fourth, and to make matters worse John suspected that Dickon, discontented himself, was also spreading disaffection among the others. In a region as little frequented as Unthank the seduction away of labour was a serious matter, but when he was spoken to about it Dickon now answered impudently, and at that once harmonious board there was a scene.

'Go and welcome, the pair of you,' John cried angrily, 'and few but me would have tholed you so long! As for that sauce-box, a bonny lot she was keeping company with the first time I set eyes on her at Umpleby if only I'd had my wits about me!' But at this Jessie only smirked and hung her head so that her neck-bone showed.

'There's company of the wrong sort at other places than Umpleby,' Dickon mumbled darkly.

'And what do you mean by that?' John blazed.

'You heard what I said,' Dickon retorted. 'I come from the Wolds, not a country you never know if it's land or water. Give me plenty of beef and mutton and I'll do without fish.'

'Yes, and you'll find yourself with a wood collar on and muck in your face if you go about giving my house a bad name!' John cried in a tone that made Dickon hold his peace, and the gloomy meal went on.

Robyn began now to wonder what had possessed him that he had ever wasted time trying to teach Polly Dacres her letters, for under that beautiful hair that the frost made stand right away from her head she had no more wits than a goose. He sometimes thought she made herself cough at will and so brought it on really, and while she was far too stupid to know what real danger was, she was fuller of imaginary fears than an egg is of meat. It put him off his wood-carving and reading alike to see her and Sally with their heads together in a corner, glancing across at Robyn, Sally with her frog's mouth and eyes perched away like a crab's on her temples and Polly with her lustrous hair. He could guess what they were whispering, because when Polly counted she did so on her fingers, and it was about how at Christmas they had sat down thirteen at the board, and Robyn had been the first to get up, and what in such cases was bound to happen. They, too, looked at him as if some awful doom hung all the time over his head, and one night, clearing away his litter after he had spoiled a good piece of wood, he overheard a few words as he passed them.

' – but Mehitabel says there's an old woman that lives at North Cave, in a hole in the river bank she lives, and never goes out in the daytime, but you have to go to her at night, and if there's somebody that wishes you ill you take something belonging to them, and she does it up in a piece of wax — '

But for the intense cold he would have spent his evenings upstairs in his belfry chamber, but the rushlight Bible was too big to read in bed, and he had turned away from its Exoduses and Isaiahs, that seemed to fill the whole world with nothing but threats and penances. He had put away his chisels and wood too, for he knew that he was untaught and that at Unthank there was none to teach him. It was an ignorant place, full of bickerings and sly back-bitings, because, except for its work, there was nothing else to do, and even when its loneliness was broken it was by these fierce swift visitations that none of them knew when to expect. Umpleby Stattis was now in a fortnight's time, yet what would his father do without him?

Humped over the fire in his own corner of the settle, with the *Pilgrim's Progress* on his knee – with the example of Christian before him and with his eyes wandering from the page to the fire and from the fire back to the page – he asked himself whether it would not be better just to set out, leaving everything as it was, without a word to any of them as to where he had gone.

9

HARD put to it as John Skyrme would have been if Robyn had packed up and departed without a word, that was not the way it came about. Robyn knew that not even Margaret Skyrme could have told him who his mother was. Only his father knew that, and to his father alone he had clung, for but for him his foster-mother's tongue would seldom have stopped where it did. Yet whenever he had asked his father this other question he had always been put off, as if like his wooden pistol anything would do to be going on with. Yet if not from his mother, where then did he get these feelings of restlessness from, these longings that passed the rest of them by did not pass him by, the hunger for fairer things, that like the amber window in Mixton church seemed somehow specially held in trust for himself? They were not things he could have asked anybody about, even if there had been anybody to ask, yet now if ever was their moment, and the opportunity too came of itself.

'Robyn,' said his father, coming in from the porch one mid-morning and shutting the outer door after him, for because of the fierce cold both doors were now kept closed, 'did you chance to hear a bang in the night?'

'No,' said Robyn, suddenly alert.

'Then you're a sound sleeper, for it woke me. I never heard one go off so like a gun before. It's the big sycamore up by the eight-acre. Wrap yourself up well and come and have a look.'

Somewhere Robyn had heard before of grown trees going off like balsam-pods in extreme frost, but he had never seen one. Muffling himself up to his freckles he got into his great-coat, and thrusting each hand well up the other sleeve for warmth he followed John Skyrme to the sycamore.

From a couple of feet above the ground, up to where the great bare branches began, the solid wood had opened as the rind of a chestnut splits on a hot hearthstone. Even at shoulder-height John was able to thrust his hand to the forearm in the deep cleft, and he cast an eye aloft to the branches, that seemed to writhe against the sky at this bursting of their heart.

'You could make a few Peters and Pauls out of that,' he said.

'Is it to come down?' Robyn asked.

'Aye, you'd better see to it. It'll keep your blood on the move. It's no matter which way you fall it. Tell Dickon to help you, for this last fortnight he's not lifted a finger without he's been told.'

For a few minutes longer Robyn stood discussing the falling of the sycamore with his father, and then stood looking down at the ground. The time was running out, and such a chance as this might not occur again. There was further business to discuss at the turnip-clamp, which was further away from the house still, and to the turnip-clamp they made their way. It was by the turnip-clamp, that Robyn had taken three days to build after that night when he had shamed himself by ringing the house-bell, that he came out with his question neck-and-crop almost before he knew it.

John Skyrme's sudden silence was that of a man who has known all along that something must be faced sooner or later. As he stood looking down on the frozen ground he seemed to have shrunk, for Robyn now easily overtopped him, and lately his troubles had come on him all at once. At last he looked up.

'Aye,' he said with a sigh, 'things cannot go on like this. You've a right to know, and I'm beginning to feel my years and cannot keep it back. We have to act according to our lights, all of us.'

'All I know is Margaret isn't my mother.'

'No, Margaret isn't your mother, yet I was never wed till I wed Margaret.'

Robyn was silent. It was no new thought to him that he was a bastard, and it came as no shock to him. But John only shook his head.

'I've never told anybody yet, and you can tell folk or not, as you please. You're asking me who your mother was. Have you never wondered about your father?' And his leathery face was as wrinkled as an old crab as he shot Robyn a glance full of wry malice.

'My father!' Robyn exclaimed, completely startled out of himself, and again John shot him the glance.

'Aye. Your father. That's what none of you knows, no, not Margaret even.'

'But aren't you my father? Do you mean I'm not a Skyrme?'

'Don't jump to ends till you've heard beginnings,' the old man replied. 'Aye, you're a Skyrme. If any of us isn't a Skyrme it ought to be me, not you. Did you ever hear tell of your Uncle Ned?'

'No – at least let me think – you once began to say something, a long time ago — '

'Nor your Uncle John?'

'I never knew I had an Uncle John,' and John Skyrme nodded, as if at least one bit of his cunning had served its end.

'It's an Uncle Ned you never had, Robyn, and an Uncle John you always had. *I'm* your Uncle John. It was my brother Ned was your father.'

Robyn had sat suddenly down on a hummock of frozen clods and straw where the clamp had been broken into. He had brought his supposed father here to ask him who his mother was, not all this about uncles and fathers. But John Skyrme, too, had sat down, and though the bitter skies might nip the living blood the dead blood of his family seemed to come to life in him again as he told his story.

'You know Margaret the same as you've always known her,' he began, prodding at the ground with his stick. 'The way you see her to-day's the way *I* decided things, not the way *she*'d have had 'em. How it began's between her and me and nobody else's business. She wanted to be mistress of Unthank, so she had to take what went with it, meaning you. Do you follow me?'

'Yes,' said the dazed Robyn.

'But she wanted a bairn of her own, and that took a bit of studying out. She wanted to know who your mother was, the same as you do. She still thinks the same as they all think, that you're one of my by-blows (for you're old enough to understand these things now). And why did I let her think so, or anything else she liked? Tell me that, Robyn Skyrme, for it's your right name I'm giving you, and always has been!'

Robyn found not a word to say.

'I did it to keep my home together and be master in my own house. There's never been a sign of one of her own. But there were *you* up and down the place, so it must be *her* that wasn't doing her part, not me. *Now* do you follow me?'

And Robyn, seated on the hummock, knew now why Margaret Skyrme had always given her tongue what tether she dared. He himself could not be in the house without perpetually reminding her, not of the truth, which was John Skyrme's sterility, but of her own infecundity and failure. Short of taking one of her own hinds to bed, which if she had done John would have thrust her out of the house, she had no way of disproving what by this time she had come to believe, and in not ceasing to harp on that cracked string John had diverted all to Robyn's head.

'But if you're my uncle,' the youth faltered, 'who was – the other?' And at that there came an alteration in John Skyrme's voice. To see his slow sad headshake one would have said that this dead brother of his was the one person in the world who had ever lived in his heart.

'Ah, Ned!' and his voice trembled. 'Robyn, you could pick me to the bones and then you wouldn't start making the man your father was! For all he was younger than me *I* was the one born to slave my life away on all this,' and he looked round. 'Twenty Unthanks wouldn't have held the likes of him, so off he goes to sea. Then when he comes back he sets up schoolmastering, in Norfolk it was, and after that he goes to London. Never still for long he wasn't, and such a picture of a man, two yards high and a face like a rose! Ah, it's me that was the wreckling, not Ned! I've heard him arguing clerks and parsons down, from balconies and market-crosses and the saddle and the mounting-stones of inns –

that was before he went for a soldier and parliament-man' – and John's voice died away, and his old eyes were fixed in front of him, as if by following their gaze others too might have seen the picture of this gallant and restless younger brother.

'So after he'd gone you were all I had, Robyn, and I had to tell Margaret you were mine to keep her in her place, but none of it'll make any difference to you, for Unthank'll be yours when the time comes. Never fear but you're a Skyrme, and after your father the best of 'em. So now you know.'

But Robyn broke excitedly out. 'But I *don't* know! That's only half of it! That's my father, and you haven't told me who my mother was!' and John looked at him fondly, for this reopening seemed to wake in him some older affection too.

'If that isn't Ned himself speaking, and him that's been dead these sixteen years come Midsummer Day!' he admired. 'My brother Ned wasn't the one to be put off with half a tale, either! But for what you ask me now, Robyn, I cannot tell you a deal about her, for I never saw her but the once, and that was before you were born. It was your father brought you to Unthank, on such a rainy night as you never saw, siling down fit to wash the Wolds away! My word, how it did rain! I can see 'em now, the two of 'em as they stood there with their horses behind 'em, hock-deep in water, for we hadn't paved the yard then — '

'Him and my mother?' Robyn cried breathlessly, but John Skyrme dropped his head again.

'Nay, poor Ned. She'd gone by that time. It was what he'd come to tell me. Him and his corporal – Simmonds his name was, Watty knew him – they were making helter-skelter for Pomfret, but there was no getting on that night. So Ned gives you and your hippings to one of the women – there wasn't any Margaret then – and they stretched themselves in front of my fire and in the morning off they pelted again.'

'But my mother!' Robyn cried, exasperated.

'I'm telling you. I never saw her but the once, though she was big with you then. It was at that inn at Lincoln next the cathedral, for Ned would have none but the best for her, and where he'd found her I cannot tell you, but she was as high a stepper as ever rode in a coach, and when he said "This is my brother," she didn't get up from the cushions she was lying on, for as I say her time was close, but she puts out her hand, and I did a thing I never did before or since – rough as I was, I kisses it — '

'What was she like?' broke from Robyn.

'She was like an apricock – but he might have picked her to wear in his buttonhole, she was that fine and small-made. Maybe my memory's going, but I cannot describe her more than she seemed such a flittermouse of a thing to have such a great belly. Her stay-laces were loose and she'd a glass of cordial in her hand in front of the fire, that Ned kept filling up for her and then drinking himself, and she'd little curls like a watter-dog, only gold – but we'd best be moving. We're catching our deaths sitting here. It's a weight off my bosom now you know it all. Let's get down to the house.'

Swinging and slapping his arms he led the way, and Robyn followed with head down behind.

For he was trying to piece together not only the fragments he had just heard, but the huge difference it all seemed suddenly to make to himself. Always he had looked upon Unthank as his home. He had already been in possession before even Margaret Skyrme came, and that doubt of bastardy under which he had lived irked nobody, for it had long been so familiar as to be wellnigh forgotten. But now he was suddenly told that Unthank was his home by adoption only. His soldier-father, hurrying through storm and mire to Pomfret siege, had dropped him there like a bundle by the way, and what was the good of telling him now that, though Margaret Skyrme had set her cap at the house with the flint lower floor and the white cobbles above, it would be his after she had gone? Suddenly he knew that he had always felt it to be no place for him. Ignorant even of his legitimacy, he had merely filled in a time of waiting there. Now there was no longer anything to wait for, and he had his liberation in his own hands. None would be the worse for his departure, they might even be the better. Why, now, should he tell any of them that he was going at all?

The breach thus made, the sea-wall itself did not crumble away more rapidly than the rest of his irresolutions. As they sat at supper that evening, John Skyrme could not open his mouth but Robyn felt himself less and less akin to him. His own father had wooed and won as high-stepping a lady as had ever ridden in a coach, but what sort of a way was this John Skyrme was treating Margaret? For the first time that he could remember he looked at the farmer with disfavour, at his foster-mother with dumb pity. First to be denied a child of her own, and then to be saddled with the cruel imposture that it was the way God had made her! No wonder she sharpened her tongue for Robyn and would shed few tears if he was out of the place!

It was little better when he turned to the others. He was weary of Dickon's sullenness, of his hole-in-the-corner philanderings with Jessie, of Jessie herself and her nape and stockinged feet and the way she seemed to stir herself inside her clothes. Polly Dacres pampered her cough and believed in ell-women, her father made a show of his distorted humour. So Robyn ate in silence, and after supper took down his greatcoat from the wall. Carrying it up to his attic he put it on his bed, with the rest of his clothing atop of it. Then, getting into bed in his stockings, he lay there planning.

Four of them were going to Umpleby, the two who

thought three times in three months enough, his uncle to get other help in their places, and himself. John would have to take the closed wagon for such unusual purchases as a journey to Umpleby always meant, and his two bad bargains would probably ride inside. But the wagon would have to go many miles round because of the frozen floods, making for Mixton and the pack-road and then casting far inland, and as Robyn reckoned it out he himself would be able to skate a very great part of the distance, saving perhaps as much as a day. Now he was trying to piece together in his head as much of the mapping of the country as he remembered.

And his reason for going to Umpleby at all, instead of remaining behind with Sim to guard the house? Ah, but he had thought of that too! He would want a little money to start off with, and he had made it his pretext that the old clockmaker's tools John had found in the chest upstairs no longer sufficed for his wood-carving, and he must have chisels and gouges of his own. But no chisels or gouges did he intend to buy. John would readily agree to his skating by the shorter way provided that at Umpleby they came together again, and in Umpleby John would look for him for perhaps half a day. Then, concluding that Robyn had already set off back, he would start for home again, with another Dickon and another Jessie beside him in the wagon. What his state of mind would be when he returned and found no Robyn was not the business of the moment. What he would think when day followed day and week week, and still his nephew did not return, only made Robyn obstinate. He continued to lie there under his greatcoat, with his head under the bedclothes for extra warmth, busily making his plans.

10

ONLY old men could call to mind a frost to compare with it. The breaching of the wall had come after nearly a fortnight of extraordinarily heavy rain, and now, like Unthank's flint and cobbles, it was neither white nor black, but a motleyed mingling of the two. To get up on a small hill and to look round was to see, wherever you looked, a marbled and magpied world, still as death now that the wind had dropped and the scurrying flaws of the ice-particles had settled again. The sun, coming up in a dazzle of cold pale splendour, only seemed to make the more heartless the brush-like striations that lay like frozen cloud-shadows over the land, and going down early, as red as an orange, it showed the waste of ice, grained and knotted in the rough places like grey wood, then planed smooth again, with here and there a straggle of hedge-top, or a roof like a raft at anchor, or the upper half of a clump of trees or the board-like body of an animal, as motionless as the swirl that had drowned it. A myriad sea-birds wheeled and floated overhead, cormorants and gulls and sheldrake and geese, and beyond the pied monotony of marbling the sullen line of the sea lay like a lapping of lead.

'Do you think you can make it before night?' John Skyrme asked anxiously, for though most folk thereabouts took to skates as naturally as a fenman takes to his stilts, he had never been much of a skater himself. He had put two horses into the wagon, and had rasped up their shoes till they struck little feathery splinters from the ice, and he held the head of one while Dickon led the other. Jessie and her bundle rode huddled up inside, and John was hoping that when they left the ice and struck the pack-road at Mixton the going would be better.

'It's a gurt way and I misdoubt if you'll do it,' he said again as Robyn glided easily by him. 'Maybe it's best you should be getting on. Have you got your lantern?'

Robyn nodded, but did not speak.

'And food to eat, and your pistol?'

'And a bag of bullets,' said Robyn.

'That's my lad. Well, be getting on your way: It's no good your wasting time with us and the sun down by four o'clock. The Swan, remember, to-morrow or the next day. Anybody'll tell you where the Swan is. So off with you and God speed,' and that was the first time Robyn had ever heard John Skyrme mention the name of God. The coverings of the wagon parted and Jessie's face looked out.

'Good-bye, Robyn, if I'm hired before I see you again—'

It eased his going a little, for 'Good-bye, Jessie, and good-bye, Dickon,' he said. Then he glided away through a gap in a hedge-top, while the wagon slipped and creaked and stumbled on.

But a furlong away he turned again. He could still see the wagon, going at a snail's pace, and John Skyrme had an uncouth and gouty look in the cloths he had swathed about his boots and the extras in which he had shawled himself. He seemed to be encouraging the horse as it slipped and dipped its head.

Not his father after all! He gave himself a shake, settled his pack, and skimmed away in a wide half-circle by the way he had come.

They had started early, the sun would not reach his wintry height for hours yet, and his chief trouble was the vagueness of that map in his head. There was none to ask, for in striking away from the hedge-tops that showed the way to Mixton he had the world to himself, and there was no wind to help or hinder. But he had only to keep the sun on his right and an eye ahead for the vagaries of the ice, and now everything he possessed was in his own keeping. In the pack on his shoulders were his shirts, his spare stockings, his best neck-cloth and his ribbed kerseys for holidays. He had money in his pocket, given him to buy tools with, and his old tools too were at the bottom of his pack, for there might be a chance of selling them. His staff was slung as Watty the fenman carried his crossbow, and this left his arms free as with the occasional clink and bite of a skate he swung along in long easy curves. For as far as he could see the ice was lightly rimed over, but otherwise as unbroken as the cream in the bowls of Margaret's dairy, and the hundreds of gulls and oyster-catchers that dotted it had a comical look, with the wiry stilts of their legs still further lengthened by their faint reflections in the ice. He was heading for Axleby, far inland from the leaden line of the sea, and at Axleby he might expect to pick up company, for Umpleby Stattis with its fairs and booths and great market and hiring was the principal event of the year, and to it people flocked not for leagues but for ridings round. He had set out confident that he could make it in a day. Now he was beginning to doubt. He didn't know what the ice might be like ahead. At Wroxton he knew he would have to cast inland again because of the narrowing of the estuary. If a skate-strap were to break that would delay him, and fifty other things might happen. He might be lucky to reach Umpleby in a day after all.

But as the sun mounted, gilding the gulls as they rested on the ice and sparkling on the frosty patches, his thoughts mounted with it. Was he not doing exactly as his own father had done, whose little finger (his uncle had said) had been of more account than all the flesh on John Skyrme's body? Running away to sea, going for a schoolmaster, contending with clerks and scholars at church-doors and market-crosses, then enlisting for a soldier – there was a romantic figure of a father to have had! Two yards high and a face like a rose, then getting himself married to a gentlewoman as dainty as an apricock-bud, with a hand that even John

Skyrme had had to stoop and kiss – away skated his imagination, too, at the thought of such a come-from. That deluge of a night when John had heard horses and the knocking at his door, and had opened it, and seen the two of them standing there, his drenched soldier-father with the corporal behind him, in a steel cap and leather jerkin belike, booted and sworded and off to Pomfret siege but stopping to leave the motherless Robyn in his brother's care – then casting themselves down to sleep for a couple of hours before the fire and then off again into the night – he seemed to have known these things all his life.

And so much for Unthank and its hinds and hired wenches, and a carping foster-mother on top of all. As he sped along like a sloop before the wind he made up pictures to himself of that inn next to Lincoln Cathedral where his mother had lain among the cushions, sipping as much of her cordial as her lover Ned had left, with her golden curls close to her head like a water-dog's, and Robyn himself inside her and the thought and wonder of Robyn a constant guessing in her eyes. Clink went his skates, twenty yards at a clink, and his thoughts rose like the gulls that hovered with their limp legs beneath them and the sunlight streaming through their strong wings. Axleby village hove ahead almost before he was aware, with its spire like Mixton's but less slender and tapering, its outlying scatter of farms, then the denser cluster of its roofs, and half its population sporting out on the ice, for the nearer you got to Umpleby the less folk seemed to have to do that day.

His first care at Axleby was to inquire what the ice was like ahead. Gliding smoothly in to where the town stood on its islet, then checking as the ice became rough with clods and stones the lads had skimmed along it, he approached the scattered fringe of people who stood looking on. Here a man had set up a brazier and was selling hot black-puddings and platters of grey peas, and to him Robyn put his question.

By keeping wide of the village, he was told, he would find all clear as far as Wroxby, but after that the pudding-seller could tell him little. He did not buy a pudding, for he would need his money for other things, but ate what he had brought from Unthank instead, and then stood to rest himself a little and look about him.

A little way out the lads had made themselves a broad slide and were following one another in a string along it. To add to their gaiety, a man was playing a hurdy-gurdy, and another had a chair on runners, on which he pushed the elder people about. More gulls than ever had flocked to the village for food, and it was as Robyn watched their constantly-changing patterns about the church spire and the dark figures that glided in and out on the ice that he suddenly heard himself spoken to from behind. Turning he saw a figure that would have been tall even if it had not been still further raised on its skates, and he was hung about like Watty the fenman with gear of one sort and another, except that it wasn't nets and ropes and bolts for his crossbow. Across his back was a sort of light wooden frame such as glaziers carry their pieces of glass in, but instead of glass it was full of flat curves and battens and templates of wood. Fastened to this was a long cylindrical roll of some kind, wrapped in a yellow oilskin sheath. A rule and a pair of callipers stuck out of his pocket, and his hat would have been a couple of feet broad if he hadn't tied a scarf round it, and then knotted it under his chin, so that sideways it hid his face completely, but when you looked at it in front it was like looking down a long shallop or scoop.

'Did I hear you asking about Wroxby just now?' this man said to Robyn, and peering into his scallop Robyn saw a curiously-shaped pair of horn-rimmed spectacles, with side-pieces like a horse's blinkers, and a great bulbous nose.

'I was asking about the ice,' said Robyn.

'You can go with your eyes shut as far as Wroxby, but

after that your best way will be to ask at the windmill. There's hay and bracken frozen in that might trip you, and they've made great holes with a pick for water.'

'Have you come that way?' Robyn asked.

'Two days ago, and back that way to-morrow, for there's nothing at the church to keep me.'

'How far is it from here before I take to the road?'

'Are you for Umpleby?' And as Robyn nodded, 'Ask them at the windmill, but you cannot miss it. You'll hear it a mile before you come to it, and if you want to make it to-night I should be pushing along.' And the man stumped up the rough bank, sat down on the ground and began to take his skates off. Robyn thrust the rest of his food back into his pocket, swung away, and took to the ice once more.

No dreams of his father's midnight arrival at Unthank or his mother sipping her cordial in front of the inn fire occupied him now, for the best part of the day was behind him and an unknown region ahead. Thoughts of purpose took their place as the gulls lost their gilding and became snowy grey and the frost seemed to tighten its grip and the only sound in his ears was the ringing and clinking of his own skates. He was looking out for Wroxby windmill, fearing to miss it in the dusk, and the sun had become a crimson globe before he saw it, its gaunt idle sails reminding him of Watty and the sea-wall, and that again setting his thoughts off, for Watty had known this corporal who had come to Unthank with his father. Simmonds his name was, and henceforward Robyn must look out for any man who bore that name. But a quarter of an hour later he was at the windmill, where they told him where the holes had been broken through the ice, and where the bracken might trip him, and at what point he had better be thinking of joining the roads again.

The sun was flattening out to a bulge when at last a hundred indications told him it was time he took his skates off. This he did under a tall finger-post from which the finger had gone, but there was no need of it, for from somewhere still a longish way ahead of him came a confused mingling of sounds. They were different from those of an ordinary pack-train, for they seemed close and more continuous, and he stamped his feet to get the feel of them again as he slung his skates round his neck and unshipped his staff. Half a mile away he saw nest-tangled elms, in so straight a line that only a road could lie behind them, and, taking a last look at the way by which he had come, he saw nothing but a flat sea of misted orange pink, with nothing to show where ice and sky met. He turned his back on it and made for the elms.

Night seemed to come suddenly with the first blink of the first lantern. The labouring of horses and jingling of bells grew steadily louder, and lights glimmered from the openings of wagon-tilts, and swung from axles and danced in the hands of the men who carried them. Occasionally a beast gave a call, and a quick pattering like rain was the tossing of a flock of sheep. Slipping through the elms and down a bank Robyn dropped to the pack-road and joined the cavalcade. For a moment he wondered whether John Skyrme had got that far yet, but he only wanted to know where John was in order to avoid him, and it would have been like looking for a needle in a haystack to seek anybody in that stream of wheels and panniers and beasts shoulder to shoulder and men who had finished one year's labour and tomorrow would be offering themselves for another. Umpleby, he judged, must be still seven or eight miles away, and suddenly he found himself wondering where he was going to sleep that night. Half these people would sleep as they journeyed and he too might beg to be allowed to creep into somebody's straw, for his ankles were beginning to stiffen and the bleak monotony of the ice had made him drowsy. So with his staff in one hand and the other on traces and tailboards he helped himself along.

Yet weary as he was, he had a sense of exhilaration, for Umpleby Stattis was like a yearly shovelling of all sorts of people together and a beginning again. Out of that heap they had sorted themselves a year ago, betaking themselves to they knew not what, and now, doing the same thing again, if what they looked for didn't happen something else certainly would. With his head nodding and his drowsy eyes on the patches of lantern-light that danced on the ground, the feathered hocks of the great horses and the turning of the wheels about him and the jingling of the bells and the voices of the unseen people in the tilts in his ears, he only knew that he had left gloomy Unthank behind him and that now his own life and story were about to begin.

II

BECAUSE John Skyrme was putting up at the Swan, Robyn decided to make his headquarters the Crooked Billet. True, the billet might have been crooked or straight or any other shape for all he knew about it till the next morning, for no courier had gone before to say that one Robyn Skyrme was on his way and that the best chamber must be made ready, and he had, in fact, lodged himself in the simplest way in the world. Tired out, dazed by the clamour and the coming and going of the lights, he had found himself in an alley, resting against a gateway, beyond which lay a yard. In the yard were many standing horses, and beyond these again a line of packed stables. Into these Robyn, with his lantern in his hand, had boldly walked. The chances were he would be taken for some ostler about the place, they could do no more than turn him out again, and in a corner was a pile of old malt-sacks. Malt-sacks or hop-pillow, by that time all was one to Robyn, and blowing his lantern out he had dreamed of Starlight. Skate from the Lincolnshire fens to within sight of the skyline of the Yorkshire Wolds in a day and you will sleep where you stretch yourself.

He was awakened by the noisy music of bells, for he knew that Umpleby minster had a different chime for every hour throughout the year, and he lay half awake on his sacks, listening to them. Then after a time he began to think about his toilet. First making sure that his money was safe, for at a hiring all sorts gather, he stretched his stiffened limbs and kicked off his coverings. In the yard people were already moving about, but no sound came from the swathed and hay-banded pump, which was ironbound, and having started with a swagger, Robyn went on. Stripping himself to his shirt and breeches he hid his pack under the malt sacks and crossed the yard. Seeing a wench with a slop bucket coming out of a doorway he pushed past her and found himself in an outer kitchen. 'Where can I wash myself?' he demanded of a hurrying lad, who jerked his head without looking at him, and that was evidently the way to do things, for in a second kitchen he found himself only one of a dozen others, standing over a trough in which the water was not yet cold, and all doing the same thing. Nobody is going to hire a man who looks as if he had slept in a ditch bottom, and to provide these conveniences was apparently a custom of the Stattis. Gillian had cut his hair again only a couple of days before, and he sluiced his head in the grey water before borrowing a comb from a man who was just finishing with it. Then, with his hair basin-cropped at the back but piled up in front in a handsome yellow wave, he sought the stable again. Breaking his fast as he dressed he stuffed his everyday clothes into his pack, hid the pack again, clapped his Sunday hat on his head, and took the streets with the best.

Already they were astir with people. Umpleby is an ancient town, not perhaps as big as Lincoln nor as busy as Kingston-upon-Hull, but with every other house a timbered inn or tavern, and with the coming of the frost braziers and grates of coal had been set outside the largest of these, with outside tables in front of their latticed windows for people to sit at. A few, muffled up to their ears, even sat at them, but most remained inside till the day was aired, looking out from the lattices and growling at the cold, or else boisterous and declaring that the more stayed away the better choice there would be for the rest. Come frost come doom the Stattis must be held, and if a few jugglers and mountebanks flinched from the cold the more money there would be to spend in the inns.

Robyn, in his best neckcloth and kerseys, made his way along the High Street to where it opened out to the great market-square. Never had he seen such a populous place, and his eyes shone at the pictures the gabled and galleried inns made, the fires in the street, the old plaster frontages and the thin smoke of the chimneys rising straight into the thinner blue of the sky. Every inn had its Swan or its Bear or its Three Scimitars slung out on its flagpole, and these flapped lazily over the booths and wooden stagings of the drolls and players, empty yet, for the sun was hardly over the rooftops and only the twin towers of the minster in the market-place caught its rays with their pinnacles. But when it came, it came in lordly fashion indeed. First a chimney-stack flushed out as red as a rose while you watched it, then a dormer window opened with a sudden flash. Along the upper casements it ran, turning tiles to red-gold and the patchy old plaster to a daisy pink, bringing people out into the streets, for nobody came to Umpleby Stattis to stay in bed. The pens in the market-place were packed with the cattle that had been there all night, and up and down the sideways lads rode horses, showing off their points while seller and buyer stood silently by. Robyn, too, watched them, comparing them with the Unthank horses, and wondering whether any of the lads had ever been set upon and blindfolded, and told that the four best must be at such-and-such a place at such-and-such a time, with halters and their feed round their necks. But as the square slowly filled, and the hinds came out with their wisps of straw in their caps and the milking-wenches with their stools, he too began to wonder for what service he was going to hire himself. He could read and write, but it wasn't for scholars that graziers and farmers came to Umpleby, and as he stood munching his bread and cheese, all that was now left of Margaret Skyrme's provision, he made a discovery, for a square-built, rubicund man who was prodding a beast in a pen stopped his prodding and called across the barrier to Robyn.

'Hast thoo not finished thy breakfast yet, lad?'

'I soon shall have,' said Robyn, which was true, and his dinner too, after which he would have to begin spending money, and the man looked at Robyn as if he would have prodded him too with his stick.

'A gurt likely lad like thoo! Fling that to the pigs, son, and come and set thy teeth into something!'

And though Robyn did not accompany him, he saw that none with his wits about him need go hungry at Umpleby Stattis, but with the right kind of look in his eye could have had six free dinners a day if he had wanted them, while as for ale and suchlike, he had only to go into an inn and sit down on a bench and his pot need never be empty.

Towards eleven o'clock a drubbing of drums and the sharp flourishes of trumpets began to rise from the High Street. The performers were assembling the passers-by for their shows. But Robyn by that time had made his way to the minster, and he was looking up at its great grey frontage when again the bells pealed out their different chime. The notes seemed to escape from the lofty louvre-boards like flights of starlings, one flight no sooner over than the next began, and even when he had entered the church, the great dim cave of its interior the vastest place he had ever set eyes on, he still could not settle his thoughts for the vibrant pealing overhead.

Then suddenly he remembered that cheek-by-jowl with the minster stood the Swan, as the inn at Lincoln too was next to the cathedral. If John Skyrme found him it might be difficult to escape from him a second time, and, looking warily this way and that, he slipped out of the minster again and made his way back along the High Street. And this time he entered the Crooked Billet by the front way, strutting in as if the place belonged to him. He shouldered his way through the crowded bars, and crossing the yard went into the stables to see whether his pack was where he had left it. The malt-sacks were undisturbed, but now in the daylight he could see that along a row of arms or brackets from which old harness hung a number of planks had been laid, and mounting by a ladder he found here as handsome a bedroom as heart could have wished. He had only to fetch his pack up, shift the ladder to another place, and he could have slept there undisturbed for a week. So he made his arrangements, and was so pleased with them that he decided to have a hot dinner in the inn's front parlour. This he did, at whose expense he did not know, for on one side of him as he ate was a farmer whose pouch seemed stuffed with gold pieces, while on the other a man was asking him how much he knew about farriery. They wanted to know where he was lodging, and he said in the house, and from so well-mannered a lad the answer did not seem to surprise them. He was asked where he had last worked and whether he had been in Umpleby before, and warned against cutpurses and pickpockets. Then they both told him not to settle himself without first letting them know, and Robyn marched out into the streets again.

All that afternoon he walked about, with an eye open, not only for John Skyrme, but for Dickon and Jessie also.

The minster bells continued to chime out the hours, he watched the jugglers and the tight-rope walkers, and supped at another inn. But he was still stiff from the skating, early in the evening he left the fair while it was still in full swing, and, mounting his ladder again, he dreamed that night of nothing at all.

The next forenoon he spent in much the same way. Again he went to the minster, but after the amber window and peaceful tombs of Mixton he found it a gaunt and overwhelming place, and he was about to leave when he saw coming out of a small corner door, hidden away like that of a vestry, a tall shambling figure with a nose like a club that somehow seemed very much at its ease in the austere and empty place. Robyn had skirted the tombstone-flags on tiptoe, almost as if his tread might have disturbed those who slept beneath, but this man was whistling softly to himself as he strode unconcernedly over them, and Robyn saw that under his greatcoat he wore a smock and a short leather apron, and his shoes were white with dust, and he carried a pair of spectacles in his hand instead of on his brow. He and Robyn were the only two people in the church, and it startled Robyn that, stopping suddenly before him, this man should address him with no more restraint in his voice than if they had met in an inn.

'So you managed to get here? You didn't miss the windmill?'

Then Robyn remembered. It was the same man who had spoken to him at Axleby, but instead of carrying his frame of wooden patterns on his back he was hatless and unburdened, and the spectacles in his hand were hinged, with small side-pieces like a horse's blinkers.

'And what are you doing here? Why aren't you out in the street watching the jugglers?' the lanky man asked in the same unhushed tones.

'I've been watching them. Then I came in here.'

'First a bit of this and then a bit of that, eh? Hasn't anybody hired you?'

'I haven't offered myself to anybody yet.'

'Do you mean you're your own master? You don't look as if you'd come to fit yourself out with hands. What can you do?' Instead of getting quieter the man's voice was raised almost as if Robyn had been deaf.

'I can read and write,' said Robyn, and the man rubbed his great blob of a nose and put on those odd spectacles to have a better look at him.

'Read and write, can you? And what's that?' And he pointed to one of the worn stones that paved the aisle.

But Robyn could make nothing of the half-obliterated letters that bordered the slab. 'O-b-i-i-t,' he spelt out, and stopped.

'You don't know Latin?'

'No.'

'You can't read that?' And this time he pointed to a lofty lancet window with a device on it, but that might have been Latin or anything else, for the spiny old text in which it was written was altogether beyond Robyn. 'And what are you by trade?'

'I've been living on a farm.'

'Run away?' the man next said, with so penetrating a look that Robyn judged it best to speak the truth.

'Yes.'

'From your parents?'

'No,' said Robyn.

'What then?' But without waiting for an answer his questioner jumped to his feet. 'But I've been sawing stone, and I can't talk with my throat full of dust. The Swan's next door. Come with me,' he said.

But Robyn did not move. 'I won't go with you to the Swan. I'll come with you to the Three Swords or the Billet.'

'Well, the Billet's a bit further, but there's worse houses,' the stone-sawer said, and Robyn followed him out of the church.

The first thing he did on reaching the Billet was to call for ale, and the next to ask Robyn whether he had had his dinner. 'Because I haven't,' he said, and shouted after the wench in a voice only a little louder than that he had used in the church. 'Make it two dinners,' and on a closer view Robyn could see that his hair was greying and that his rounded club of a nose had little pittings like a pepper-box. Then he set about his questioning of Robyn again.

His name, he said, was Maas, and he was a church-mason, but as he talked Robyn gathered that he was rather more than an ordinary labourer, for he talked about architecture, too, as if he knew all about it, and somehow Robyn didn't think he was boasting. His having no regular employment seemed further to bear him out, for he had the air of being his own master, a take-it-or-leave-it sort of air, as if it was the place of others to come to him and not his to go running about after them. With so much churchware ravaged and stolen and destroyed, he said, but happier days now to look forward to, he earned good wages, patching, restoring, advising, moving from place to place, and he kept his dusty throat clear too, for he knew almost as much about inns as he did about churches. All this he told Robyn as they ate, and then asked him whether he had a steady head for heights.

'I think so,' said Robyn.

'Could you climb a steeple and set a weathercock?'

Robyn had to admit that he had never set a weathercock.

'Because,' said mason Maas, 'it's roofs begin to make me think I'm not the man I was. There's an outside staircase at Ely I don't fancy now the same as I used to. You must be fond of churches to go sitting in them when there's play-acting to be seen for nothing.'

So Robyn told him about Mixton church, and the figures

on the tomb he had tried to copy in wood, and again the mason put on his spectacles to have another look at him.

'A lady on a tomb did you say? That's what I've been doing this very morning here in Umpleby. Sawing eighteen inches out of her middle like cutting a sausage in two, and a new block to fit in and the draperies to copy so that but for the colour you wouldn't know the difference. Ah, they send for Hendryk Maas when there's a delicate job like that to do! Mixton did you say? Whose tomb is it?'

'Robertus something — '

'I must have a look at it when I'm next that way. It's only wood you carve? Not stone?'

'Only wood,' and the mason took a deep draught and then shook his head in violent disapproval.

'Wasting your time like that! It's stones, that'll last for centuries, that's a man's job! And you draw too?'

'Only my own way. I haven't been taught.'

'Then it may be you'd have the less to unlearn. There's too many that's been taught a deal too much, and as for your only cutting wood, if the one's got its home in you the other's somewhere about. And you're here in Umpleby for the hiring?'

And Robyn had had enough of turnip-clamps and ploughing and carrying food to the cattle and doing women's work about the house when there was nothing to do out of doors. In the parlour of the Crooked Billet that afternoon, with John Skyrme anxiously waiting for him at the Swan, he signed on with Hendryk Maas for a year.

12

FOR the learning of his trade he could have done no better thing, but after that the questions began. Hendryk Maas had travelled in Brabant and the Low Countries, France,

Germany, and even as far as Bavaria, but he was a man of a cantankerous and unyielding disposition, and in every one of these places he had managed to pick a quarrel with the various Guilds and their dignitaries. So before Robyn as much as knew what a Guild was, there was Hendryk already cramming it down his throat that all such corporate bodies had it as their aim and end to keep down the craftsman whose heart was in his job.

'Have nothing to do with them,' he was telling Robyn before he had known him a day. 'If you haven't got a counsellor inside you that'll tell you better than they can, let it alone and shake a bowl for pennies. Guildhalls and gold plate and charters and burgomasters with their fur caps and chains of office are no business of yours. Such as cannot stand on their own feet are always the best at propping one another up, and when they have got you fast and bound they won't pay you the wages I'll pay you if you're worth it and heed what I say.'

The result of all this was that though, as he boasted, he never lacked employment, it was never put in his way, but he had to bestir himself to get it. Such, indeed, was his distrust of those who sat at the high tables that he would sometimes fling their work back in their faces rather than accept it at their hands, and if deans and chapters thought they knew more about the fabric of a church than Hendryk Maas did let them take their patronage somewhere else and leave him alone.

It was in a sort of penthouse tucked away behind the minster that the craft and mystery of Robyn's new trade was unveiled to him, with the ground shoe-deep in dust, and half-dressed blocks of stone lying about, and oddments in need of replacement or repair lifted down from their gutters or pinnacles, broken finials and gargoyles and fractured capitals and waterworn gutters. The tools he had hitherto used seemed effeminate by the side of Hendryk's great pudding-shaped mallets and steel straightedges and stone-chisels and dusty templates and squares, and in his new enthusiasm it seemed to him that wood was only good to light fires with. In the chancel Hendryk had lifted a sort of mortuary-sheet from the stone lady, showing the two severed ends of her, her wimpled head and the pious folds about her toes and the gap of her amputated middle. In the penthouse was the piece that had been taken out, side by side with the roughly dressed block that was to replace it, with the points for the dowellings already marked on its ends. And for all one side of the shed lay open to the bitter weather, Robyn felt the blood tingling in his veins with excitement.

But it was the great rolls of drawings that set his blue eyes bulging, for here was the heart of the mystery itself. Curled up in his hands or held down on a stone block by other stones, here at last was the answer to what he had tried to do by his own lights at the cleared end of the Unthank table. So you didn't just get a piece of wood and a chisel and shut your eyes and hope for the best! It wasn't enough to want to do it and it forthwith came alive in the death-like stone! You had to square and measure, and do figures in your head, for all the world as if you had been doing John Skyrme's accounts! And then, when you had done all this, you had to set it aside as if it had never been! From drawing to drawing he turned, egg-shaped angels' heads, carefully-centred moulding-sections, foliated crockets, squared-up details, the pattern of a mitre. It all seemed endless, and he sighed, but Hendryk Maas encouraged him as he drilled holes all over his stone block till it began to resemble his own pepper-box of a nose.

'I can teach you what the Guilds can't for all their gold plate and banketting,' he said. 'It's *me* that's the free mason, not them! Everything to themselves they want to keep, but *I* haven't worked in Bruges and Louvain and Nuremburg and Caen for nothing! *I* find my own work! *I* write my letters ahead, and when *I'm* ready it's waiting for me, and show me your cap-in-hand Guildsman who can say as much!'

So Umpleby Stattis came and went, with its thronged and lighted streets at night, its mountebanks and its packed inns, its buying and selling of beasts and pocket-picking and harlotry. Its crowds melted away again as hinds and cowmen and carters and dairy-wenches left by other directions than those by which they had come. Not a soul from Unthank did Robyn catch as much as a glimpse of, and the Swans and Scimitars came down from their flagstaffs, and Hendryk put a chisel into his hand and gave him a piece of stone and told him to do what he liked with it while he worked at the middle of the lady. When it was finished, Robyn helped him to carry it back to the chancel, where its drapery fitted as exactly as if nothing had been taken away, and then, his job at Umpleby finished, Hendryk prepared to pack up, and looked again at Robyn.

'Well? Are you still of the same mind?' he asked. 'There's still time to think again if you're not.'

'I don't want to think again,' said Robyn.

'Just as it comes, the rough with the smooth?'

'Yes,' said Robyn.

'Then we'll sleep in Umpleby to-night and to-morrow we'll be taking the road.'

'Where do we go next?' Robyn asked.

'We're crossing to Yorkshire. We're for Holderness,' Hendryk replied.

For some reason these last words did not immediately chill Robyn. First they had to settle themselves in, and the chill came a couple of hours later, when they had finished their supper at the Billet, and Hendryk, his tools fetched away from the minster and packed on his flat hand-cart in the yard, sat with his long shambling legs stretched out to the fire. Robyn spoke in a subdued voice.

'Whereabouts are we going in Holderness?'

'To Mocklington. Perpendicular, and there's a steeple for you! It's almost tall enough to see from here, and in a high wind it swings twelve feet at the top for all its piercings. It makes my head swim to think of it.'

'I've never been to Holderness. What's it like?'

'It's not a deal different from where you say you come from. As flat as a slab, but it's all reformed church there, so they haven't fared as badly as some. It's when you get north, where the abbeys and monasteries used to be, you find the water coming into your eyes,' and though at that moment Robyn was thinking of nothing less than of churches and their steeples he continued to ask his questions about Holderness.

For it all came back the more freshly that he had begun to forget it. Yet there is no going through life if every step you take is going to be a fear, and without confessing anything to Hendryk he still went on with his questions about this place Mocklington, what the farming was like there and similar matters, till Hendryk, with his after-supper drowsiness coming on, jerked himself awake again and asked what the catechism was all about.

'We're starting on a north window this time,' he said. 'They had terrible great gales there last spring, and it was blown in, and that's as much as I can tell you till I've seen it.'

'Is it anywhere near Withernsea?'

'As near as makes no matter.'

'And Hornsea?'

'They're all adjacent.'

'Isn't there a Queen of Holderness?'

'Not that I've ever heard tell of.'

'And a Prince of Withernsea?' And Hendryk woke up.

'Eh? Ah, I have you! You've been listening to foolish tales somewhere. There might be a few odd Earls of Hornsea, and Dukes of Spurn too, if it comes to that, but I haven't been round those parts lately. I did hear some talk about one of them being dead,' and suddenly Hendryk raised his voice for the special mixture he always treated himself to when he had finished a job. The drawer brought the mixture. Whatever else there was in it, it contained rum, and as its fragrance spread through the parlour Robyn ceased for a time to question.

But now that he had bound himself to Hendryk many things would have to come out sooner or later, and to get a few of them over now would both ease his own breast and stop Hendryk from asking at some future date why he hadn't told him before. Again he cleared his throat.

'They say their real name's Fyfe.'

'Whose real name's Fyfe?'

'Those that we're talking about,' and Hendryk looked at him as he had looked when he had asked him so suddenly whether he had run away from his parents.

'You've something on your mind, lad,' he said. 'Out with it.'

'Who told you the one that called himself the Prince of Withernsea was dead?'

'I cannot call to mind. Getting about I hear a lot of gossip,' and Robyn's voice suddenly jumped a note.

'And not only him. The other's dead too!'

'What ails you? What other?'

'The one they unburied again and took away in a kelp-cart.'

Hendryk finished his mixture and immediately called for another. There was silence till it came, and then Hendryk said, 'Oh. They took him away in a kelp-cart, did they?'

'You knew?'

'No, I didn't know, but hadn't you better tell me?'

So with things as far as that out the rest had to come, and in the lately-crowded parlour, with the haunting smell of the rum in his nostrils, Robyn told all. The mixture was a hot one, but it was half cold before Hendryk spoke again.

'So that's why you left your home?'

'It's some of it,' said Robyn tremulously, and Hendryk placed his stone-hardened hand on his knee.

'Then just try to forget about it, lad. It's true there's all sorts about in these times, but I didn't know it was as bad as that. You learn your trade, and stick to me, and nobody'll meddle with us.'

'You'd have thought they wouldn't meddle with old Nicholas, but you can't say that when there he was, lying in the yard — '

But he got no further. Hendryk jumped as if he had been shot.

'Old *who*?'

'Old Nicholas the pedlar – there he was lying with his throat cut, and his clothes all open, and – and – I can't tell you —'

'Nicholas the . . . here, have a drink of this!' And Hendryk forced the lukewarm rum down Robyn's throat. 'Drawer!' he called, and not till the drawer had gone did he turn to Robyn again.

'There. There's *schiedam* in that too. Hold up. Now you're better. Old Nicholas! And you say all this was at this place Unthank?'

'Yes,' Robyn faltered.

'Old Nicholas! That I've tramped scores and scores of miles with, and me wondering what had become of him! A quiet simple old man like him! That comes of people getting together in guilds and murdering gangs. Old Nicholas! . . . From York to Lincoln I've walked with him one time and another, talking about anything to pass the time! He'd an ague once, and first I put his budget on my cart, and then him after it, and half a day I pushed him. Old Nicholas! . . . But don't come to Holderness if that's the way you feel. I've got to go, but I can meet you on a date somewhere else. Not that they'd think of looking for you on their own doorsteps, but do as you feel. There's no indenture to break. With a Guild you'd have had an indenture and catchpoles set on you, by the neck they'd have had you, but you're free of all that with me. So do as you like. Old Nicholas! It's a queer world, when things like that can happen in it — '

And whether it was having told Hendryk, or however it was, Robyn felt better. Come what may, a man must go where his work is, and if it takes him into danger, so much the more reason why he should keep his eyes open and his wits about him. In his fifteenth year he was as big and strong as any eighteen, and with a father who had plunged through rain and mire to face his death at Pomfret siege he would have been ashamed to let Hendryk Maas go forward into Holderness while he lagged behind. At Unthank, uninstructed and dispirited, he had fumbled about with his bits of wood as Sim Dacres had cobbled up his old straps and oddments of iron; but now he felt himself face to face with the trade to labour at which he had been brought into the world. Though Hendryk might be a boastful master he was a grand one, and even if his lot had not cast him for a soldier he might yet be able to look round before he died and say that he, Robyn Skyrme, had done thus and thus.

That night he slept on his harness shelf in the Crooked Billet stables for the last time. Betimes the next morning he had taken one handle of a tool-laden two-wheeled flat cart, with Hendryk Maas at the other, and the two of them were making for the river at North Cave, a ferry to Goole on the other side, and so by the icebound roads to Holderness.

13

HENDRYK had said that Holderness was very like his own country, but except for its unbroken flatness one saw little resemblance. There was no sea with its distant line of silver or lead, and for so many miles before you came to it did you see Mocklington's great perforated steeple swinging its twelve feet that your eyes grew weary of the sight of it. Nor was Mocklington itself any more attractive when you got there. A straight road ran through it in an apparently endless line to the east, another endless road crossed it from north to south, the church stood where the two met, and a few lesser streets filled up the corners. So that, Robyn mused, was Mocklington-in-Holderness. There were a few farms, and away back in James's time somebody had tried to work for coal there, but it was little more than a surface seam, they had given it up, the potholes had been baulked over again, and the colliers had returned to their farms.

Hendryk and Robyn made straight for the church, not to see what their work was to be, but first to get rid of the encumbrance of their cart. Having done this they found an inn in North Street, Hendryk spruced himself up to go and see the prebend in authority, and Robyn, hoping his appearance was that of a mason born, awaited his return in the inn.

But he was not Robin Skyrme now. At his own request, made while Mocklington spire was still a needle on the skyline, he had decided to be Richard Eccles. He would have been Richard Maas, which would have been easier to answer to, except that it was known at the church that Hendryk had no son, and as for passing himself off as his nephew, he had had enough of uncles whom he had supposed to be fathers. So here Richard Eccles was, in a country whose evil name spread far away into Lincolnshire, and his hand stole to the pistol in his pocket. A few sullen-looking people entered the inn and went out again, no doubt to see who the foreigner was, and Robyn, forgetting his mistake about the one-eyed chairman in Mixton church, kept his back to them and himself to himself. It is not difficult to imagine faces as dishonest or honest, at our pleasure. It seemed to Robyn that these men of Mocklington must have been left over from the coal-pits, creeping back into them again when night fell. But Hendryk, when he returned, seemed to bear them no ill-will, and his Richard this and Richard that as night fell and they began to drop in in numbers made Robyn glad he had Hendryk at his side.

Nevertheless, it was several evenings before he was able to shake off the feeling that the Mocklington men, if not ruffians themselves, were still privy to some hushed conspiracy, and this only left him with the unfolding of the work there was to do at the church.

For see Hendryk set about a job when he had his feud with the Guilds to prick him on! They found the scaffolding already up by the north door when they reached the church that morning, and as they mounted the ladder to the staging the wind hummed through the great perforated steeple as if it had been a lyre. In the days that followed, Robyn's job was to fetch and carry, and while Hendryk went over the fractured stone ribs and veinings with a piece of chalk, determining which must be excised, up and down the ladders Robyn trotted, carrying this tool or that, but keenest of all to see a master stonecutter buckling to his job. As there had been a penthouse behind Umpleby minster, so here beyond the close was a builder's shed with a great working-table. Down to this Robyn carried the stone cusps and interlacings as Hendryk removed them, checking each by drawing and rule and setting it by the new cube or oblong that was to replace it. The great gap of the window began to look like a yawning jaw from which Hendryk had extracted the teeth, and with the removal of the last stump the work began.

And as it progressed it began slowly to dawn upon Robyn that he had seen far more lawlessness among the Unthank sandhills than in this dreaded region where it was supposed to have its home. As day followed day, and the long frost broke, and still Hendryk cut and channelled and ran his templates up and down, that cheerless inn in North Street became a thousand times more desirable at night than his bed on the shelf among the Crooked Billet harness. If these Mocklington men had secret knowledge of wicked deeds they kept their knowledge to themselves, and they certainly did not sleep down the pits, for Robyn saw them going in at their own doors and caught glimpses of their suppers waiting for them on the tables. Hendryk, with his cordial beside him, spent his evenings in the inn parlour, writing letters for more work ahead. These he entrusted to the licensed carrier or to some traveller who chanced to be journeying that way, for with the authority of the Church behind them his letters had a smack as it were of sanctity, and certain of the local men even made up to him for the sake of the odds-and-ends of work he was able to put in their way. So for nearly eight weeks the restoration went forward. The day came when Hendryk gave orders for the scaffolding to be taken down. Lacking only its glass, the new window stood out in its renovated and symmetrical whiteness, and Hendryk, with his tools already packed up on his cart again, stood looking up at it. Then he gave an odd sigh.

'The glass goes first, and the stone lasts longest, but they'll both see our time out,' he said. 'It isn't a lot to look at maybe, but the little bit we know goes up there, so you can call it a bit of us, and that's as much as the best or the worst of us can say. The main is that we should have done our best. Now let's go and settle up at the inn.'

So, with the anemones out in the hedge bottoms, and the birds building too, and no saying which swung the more merrily, the catkins on the twigs or the lambs' tails in the fields, they took the road again.

With the thinning away of Mocklington's spire behind them no blither lad than Robyn was now had ever pushed a handcart. He sang or recited aloud just whatever came into his head, bits of songs he had learned from Sim Dacres or scraps from *The Pilgrim's Progress*, for he wished Hendryk to notice that he had done his share of reading too, and he was now Robyn Skyrme again, for with Mocklington out of sight behind them the Richard Eccles had been dropped. But with their faces set north, Hendryk was moody, and had no eyes for the birds' nests that Robyn was so quick to spy, and only said '*Follow the Horses,* marry!' as the tools and templates on their flat cart rattled like a tinker's van. And then one day Robyn happened to chant something from The Register, for grave or gay was all one to him, and to his surprise Hendryk cut him short.

'Have done! Where did you come by that terrible thing?' and Robyn stopped.

'It's in one of the books my father left me,' he said, for he had long since come to the conclusion that those half dozen books at Unthank could only have been left there by Ned Skyrme, and now it was Hendryk who muttered from The Register as they walked.

> '*When Mary Swanton met her death*
> *We sighed for good Elizabeth —*

'–and well they might, or for Henry or Mary or any of them, whatever they called themselves, for what one of them didn't lay flat the next did, with a Lord Protector to finish the job! –

> '*When Giles and Grey gave up the breath*
> *We groaned for Queen Elizabeth —*

'– wait till we get a bit further north! You'll see what the likes of us set up, for them and their soldiery to fetch down again! You wait for what I'll show you!' And it was now he who went on muttering to himself that terrible Smithfield litany that Robyn had so unthinkingly begun.

'Have you ever been to Pomfret?' Robyn asked, to

take his mind off it, but again Hendryk gave him a short answer.

'Pomfret? What's Pomfret to do with it? Pomfret's a castle. I'm talking about monasteries and abbeys.'

'My father was at Pomfret,' said Robyn.

'Then for all I know your father was another of them, kingsman or malignant, what care I? It isn't churches but guildhalls they ought to have destroyed! –

'When fire James Snell delivereth
We longed for our Elizabeth —

'–but there's still men it takes more than an army to stop, so we'll talk about something else. It's time somebody taught you your Latin declensions,' and into the Latin declensions he straightway plunged.

So day followed day and inn inn at night as they travelled ever further north, towards the broad abbey-lands; and of Byland or Jervaulx, Rievaulx or Fountains, Robyn was never quite sure which they lighted on first, and it was then that he saw what Hendryk meant by his bitter talk of the destruction wrought by kings and queens. For they came upon the first of them suddenly, and it was a melancholy sight, breasting a pleasant hill that raised the vale below, suddenly to see in the middle distance those mangled stones that had once been a fane. Hendryk, savagely tearing his own wounds open again, would seize him roughly by the arm or thrust him forward, as if it had been Robyn's own doing, and the less there remained the more he lifted up his voice, for the very stones had been carted away to mend the miry roads or patch up an outhouse wall. In chancels sapling trees had already taken a flourishing hold. Nettles and weeds had lodged in the niches and great claps of dung fouled the dortoir floors. The cattle lowed through what was left of the cloister arches, and where the tomb-flags had been prised up were sumps of mud. Unweathered and harsh, even the ivy had hardly begun to mantle the destruction over, and at Byland a tall stub of arch looked like a bowed neck, still stiff and waiting after its head had gone. As well seek to mend the rents in an angry sky as those former coral-aisles of praise each fragment of which (Hendryk said) had been the life of a man, and Robyn had to drag him away, but even then he would sit suddenly down by the roadside, and tell Robyn to go ahead and he would catch him up bye and bye.

And the desolation that overspread the abbey-lands seemed to have broken some happy spell, for now something seemed to have happened to Hendryk's letters ahead. At first he said nothing about this to Robyn, but for a couple of days perhaps would cheer him up with the promise of work at the end of them, when they would be able to settle themselves down again as they had settled down at Mocklington, busy all day and resting in their inn at night, for Hendryk was paying for everything, and his money was beginning to run low, and Robyn sometimes thought he could have lived on what Hendryk spent on his cordials and mixtures at the inns. But when they reached their journey's end, Hendryk would put on his decent clothes to wait on the incumbent or whoever the official might be, and lo, Robyn could tell by his face the moment he entered again that something had gone amiss. Unable to blame Robyn, he took the blame upon himself that apparently some letter had not come to hand, and tried to explain it away. It was the first time it had happened, he said, and when you came to think of the uncertainty of the times, and the state of the roads, and how letters must be as multitudinous as birds on the wing, it was no miracle that a letter now and then failed to reach its destination. It would only have been a short job, anyway, he said, and three or four other letters had been despatched well ahead. So off they would trudge again.

Nor did Robyn at first notice the way in which Hendryk began to return to the subject of the Guilds, and always with a fresh rancour. There was only one thing worse than the enmity of the Guilds, he said, and that was when they came smiling to you and tried to cozen you with their friendships, and now it did not take Robyn quite so long to guess what was the matter. Wherever Hendryk now went he found that the Guild men had been before him. Either plans had been changed or they had not been as solidly grounded as Hendryk had led Robyn to suppose, but it all came to the same thing: while the Guild-men were busily at work in the shops and sheds Robyn and Hendryk were on the roads with their flat cart of tools. And so for the two of them the hard times began.

Not once or twice that spring, but often and often, it was the same tale. They must live, Hendryk must either mend walls or slate roofs for small men of no account or go hungry, and Robyn, also casting about to find what occupation he could at the nearest farm, sighed for Unthank among these hard Yorkshire folk. He wondered who John Skyrme had found at Umpleby Stattis and taken back with him in place of Dickon and Jessie, what Margaret and Mehitabel were doing, and how Starlight was getting on in his stall. But Hendryk would admit no defeat. His constant burden was now York. At York they would look at none but the best men, he said, and if his name wasn't as well known there as the archbishop's it ought to be. And such was his resilience of spirit, and so wanton did it seem to say anything to throw cold water on his hopes, that there were times when Robyn almost believed him, for there could be no doubt he was a prince among stone-cutters if only the Guilds would have stayed their all-powerful hands.

But there came a morning when Hendryk, settling their reckoning at an inn where their lodging had been hardly third-rate, found himself some shillings short. It was indeed a question whether he would not have to pledge his most precious possession, his pointing-instrument; but Robyn had not yet touched the money John Skyrme had given him to buy wood-chisels with. It lay in a bladder at the bottom of his pack. Out it came, and at the sight of it Hendryk gave him a piercing look, but took the money without a word. The word did not come till that afternoon, when they were far on the road again. Then:

'Robyn,' he said, 'that was a lesson you taught me this morning.'

As Robyn, too, had been thinking things over he did not reply, and Hendryk went on.

'It isn't right masters should lien on their prentices for money, and I know my drinking stands me in a good deal. I owe you four shillings. You shall have it back, never fear. But I'll drink no more till we're settled in a proper job at York.'

But Robyn now had two things on his mind. The first of them was what Hendryk, who had paid so handsomely for everything, must think of him for having had money all this time he had said nothing about. And the second was whether the Guilds were not after all in the right of it, and he would not have done better to bind himself apprentice like everybody else than to start out as a journeyman with a guide as headstrong as Hendryk Maas.

14

So the high summer wore on, with its day-by-day difficulties solving themselves as somehow they do, and even if they don't we somehow still survive them. The hours of darkness were short, and there were times when work failed altogether, but there was usually a barn or haystack to sleep under, and if the dews chilled them they slept by day and did their walking by night. Then something else would turn up, a week's work at a quarry perhaps or a job carting stone, and to sleep out or walk by night in the pick of the year is to save lodging-money, and Robyn had his four shillings back, and was told he was not to lend Hendryk any more no matter what the deadlock seemed to be. But the autumn had set in when at last they reached York, and Hendryk wheeled his cart into an inn yard, and then strode into the inn, and called for hot water and gave himself such a sluicing as he had not had for months, and then ordered Robyn straight to bed, for it was the last he would see of Hendryk Maas that evening.

It was indeed the last he saw of him till ten o'clock the next morning. What old friends he had been hunting up Robyn did not know, but one look at Hendryk's face told him that the bad days were over. He was in his working clothes again and his great plain face was all alight as he stood by Robyn's bedside. For had he not told Robyn so? Had he not said that in York their troubles would be at an end? Let the ignorant scoff at the name of Hendryk Maas, who had learned his trade in Louvain and Bruges, Chartres and Caen! The truly great knew better, and here in York there was work the year through, work that never stopped, or with a fabric such as York's to serve what mattered a few generations of men? He flung Robyn's working clothes on the bed too.

'Up, you ragged woodcarver, up, my cock-robin, and earn your breadcrumbs!' he exulted, for he had had a nip of the cordial already. 'When Hendryk Maas says a thing is so, so it is, and Amen and Amen! On with your clothes, my bold Robyn, and come and see what I'm going to show you — '

The great stoneyard to which Robyn was taken that morning was not in the precincts, but some little distance away, on the other side of Bootham Bar, and that Hendryk had not lied even Robyn knew by the great shout that went up at the sight of his loose double-jointed figure and his bulb of a nose with the hinged spectacles above it. The York men left their blocks and buckets and saws and stone-planes to flock round him, mobbing and embracing him, for not all of them were English, and Robyn forgot his loose ways with letters and the hole in the pocket where he kept his money, for receptions such as that cannot be bought. He spent that morning in going round with Hendryk from block to bench and from bench to turntable, sometimes called a young runagate and sometimes the trimmest lad who ever stepped, and then Hendryk went to the inn to lie down, for he had high functionaries to see later in the day.

And here, under Hendryk, Robyn at last set about the learning of his trade.

But they had gained the shelter of York with only a few weeks to spare, for one afternoon the skies grew heavy as lead, and Robyn shivered to think of the haystacks and hedges as over the great city winter set in, this time with snow. Snow shuttering down from the roofs in heavy sheets blocked the streets. It turned the grey old walls into mural crowns, with ever more snow in suspension ready to fall. The great west towers of the minster were pencilled and picked out like ermine against the sky, and the chopped-off heads of the traitors that pinnacled the grim castle were capped with grotesque wintry nightcaps. Hardly within memory had there been such a snow, but Robyn and Hendryk were now snugly within doors, Robyn at a vast oblong drawing-table with trued-up edges, against which he set his T-squares and angles, with scale and compasses to measure by and Hendryk's great spoonbill of a nose thrust over his shoulder, for the Guilds would have set Robyn to carrying buckets or hauling on lifting-tackle, but when Hendryk Maas took a pupil he took a son. Clerks and messengers and others from the cathedral would present themselves in the doorway, stamp the snow from their boots, and hand Hendryk rolls and parcels of old plans and drawings, and then off Robyn would have to pack, for his drawing-table would be required, and Hendryk would have hardly a word to spare for him for the rest of that day. But once he was taken across to the private office of the minster architect himself, where the records and registers were kept, and for the whole of that night he dreamed of winding turret stairs, and old doors that he had to stoop to get into, and his own future, like a promised land before him, and the high privilege that was already his.

The greater working-place in which he now began to spend his days was in effect divided into two, though there was no actual division. At the quieter end of it sat Hendryk and a couple of other draughtsmen, though these two were not always the same, and here was comparative quiet, and in the short afternoons lights burned early, and if any detail was to finish these lights were sometimes to be seen as late as seven o'clock in the evening. But beyond a wooden screen lay the great workshop itself, and here was nothing but busy noise as long as the daylight lasted. Overhead ran tackle for the lifting of blocks, and this meant a constant rattling of chains and cries of 'Easy, steady,' and men at ropes, and the light clash of the falling chains as the block was cast off again. At the extreme end the ground had been guttered into a kind of trough, for here was the rushing of water from hoses and the gritting of the round grinding-irons in the sand as some great oblong of stone was brought to a true surface. Stone-saws rasped harshly, and the planing machine ceased suddenly as the groove or channel ended, and the work began its reverse journey, and the clinking of chisels was like an aviary, and the drill whirred, and there were other noises too, for though the cathedral work came first, secular work too went on, and in the great yard outside carts came and went, with slating for roofs and piping for drains and great brick-stacks for other purposes. And Robyn discovered that if he would learn his trade he must learn the men who did these things too, and one by one he began to know them, and how things were done in other yards, across the seas perhaps, and about Hendryk too, not always to his advantage. For many of these too were Guild men, who said that Hendryk might have his gifts, but the most gifted of men must come to heel sooner or later. Then Robyn would defend Hendryk, but experienced Dutchmen or Walloons would tell him to wait and see, and some of these Robyn liked but some he didn't, but it was all experience, and already he was casting about in all this for a private little corner where he could make a small world of his own.

For even at Unthank he had wondered why they didn't sometimes put a field-mouse into the foliations of their courses or capitals, or a snail with its whorl of a shell, or some other peeping creeping thing, instead of always grinning masks and imps, that always seemed to bring the devil into the church; and as his fingers grew more skilled and obedient he would furtively try his hand at some such thing, showing his idea only to Hendryk. But Hendryk always shook his head.

'Don't let Mechlin Tom or any of the Guild men see them. Alter a settled line by a hairsbreadth and you'll have the roof down on your head. What's this one now?'

'A squirrel wringing its tail,' said Robyn.

'A squirrel doing what?'

'Squeezing the water out of its tail with its hands. Haven't you seen them?' and Hendryk exclaimed with delight.

'It's the truth I'd never noticed! Come to think of it, what else would they do? Their tails are for balance. Get 'em wet and they wouldn't be able to hop about as free as you and me, eh? To be sure they've the sense to wring their tails, for comfort too – but don't let the Guilds know! To think of all the squirrels I've seen and never noticed a little thing like that!'

But as the winter wore on, though no more snow came, Robyn began to be burdened with other thoughts too. Only lately had there begun to haunt him again a picture he had last seen now almost a year ago, of a wide and winter-bound landscape, and a tilt-cart with chains round its wheels, and two labouring horses with their shoes newly rasped up for a better hold on the ice, and John Skyrme with his legs swathed like a gouty man's, and Jessie Byers putting aside the tilt-sheet to call out 'Good-bye, Robyn, if I'm hired at Umpleby before I see you!' He had promised to meet his uncle at the Swan, but he had looked out for him in Umpleby only to avoid him, and the Stattis had been over before he had given any of them another thought. But now it returned. There they would all be, sitting in the hall of an evening, at first telling one another that he would be back to-morrow, then falling into silences, and John Skyrme listening on the settle and suddenly getting up to walk about, and Margaret biting her lip that ever she had mocked him about bolting the doors, and a hundred other disturbing pictures. What had the hay been like that year, and had the stacks been left alone? Had any of them set out to find him? What were all these tales of bodies found by roadsides, and hurried inquests and hasty shovellings away? What kind of a household had Robyn, so busy now with his pencil and rule and squirrels, left behind to mourn him as dead?

Then one day, stirred to compunction, he sat down to write a letter. Nobody at Unthank would be able to read it – if Polly Dacres tried to do so she would be sure to get it wrong – but a letter at Unthank would be like the ground opening under their feet and they would get it read one way or another. But he had just got into his letter when he smelt the smell of rum over his shoulder and heard Hendryk's voice.

'What's to do now, Robyn? Are you turning clerk? Or is it that trim lass of Holcroft's who brought him in the hot trotters the other day?'

'I didn't see any lass bringing Holcroft trotters,' said Robyn, but Hendryk only grinned.

'Little difference that makes if they see you first! Once they start casting their eyes about — '

'I was writing to my uncle,' said Robyn, wishing Hendryk would go away, but Hendryk was in a gossiping mood.

'Him you used to live with? And a very proper thing too. How did you think of sending it?' but without waiting for an answer he went on. 'You remember when we were in Mocklington I wrote some letters that never came to hand? I've never stopped thinking about that. It's true he was a man I didn't know well, but he said he was coming up north and I thought no more about it. I've often wondered whether it was wise to trust him.'

'Was that the letter about the rainwater-heads at Upthorp?'

'That was the one of 'em.'

'And you think he mightn't have delivered it?'

'I don't know what to think. It never got there. Best send that you're writing by the proper mail-carrier. Nobody else is allowed to ride post with them.'

But Robyn did not write his letter, for somehow he found it too difficult. Whatever harm was done was done, and he wished Hendryk had not seen him writing it. Hendryk himself, however, returned to the miscarriage of his own letter to Upthorp that very same night. They lodged together in a narrow street near Monk Bar, sharing the same chamber and the same candle, which stood by Hendryk's bedside, for he frequently took a book to bed to read before he went to sleep. That night, however, he just talked to Robyn across the room, and as Robyn heard enough of his voice during the day he was just settling himself again to sleep when again the question of the missing letter came up.

'Yes, I begin to misdoubt me about that man,' said Hendryk, as if he had been thinking of nothing else ever since.

'It wasn't a letter that 'ld be any good to anybody else, even if they opened and read it. It'll be a lesson to me for another time. Yet he was a fair-spoken man too. Did I tell you? It was at Mocklington, when we were working on that north window. He asked me something civil about what style we called it, and I answered the way we do, telling him it was English Perpendicular, and I met him again that same evening over a glass, and I had the letter in my pocket, so I handed it to him — '

But for some reason or other Robyn sat suddenly up in bed. 'What was he like to look at?' he asked, and Hendryk drowsily considered it.

'Well, he'd a fur cap with flaps tied down over his ears, and a frieze coat trimmed with fur, for you remember how bitter cold it was, and his boots were lined with fur at the top too — '

'That's his furs, not him,' said Robyn impatiently.

'So it is, but you don't see a deal of a man when he's wrapped up like that. How much of me do you see when I clap my hat down on my cheeks and tie my neckcloth over it? He'd a thin, lawyerish sort of face, with hanks of grey hair hanging down his cheeks, very learned and respectable-looking. I don't set up to notice everybody the way you notice squirrels,' and out went the candle, and Robyn heard the creaking of his bed as he rolled over.

But Robyn could not sleep. It was true that Hendryk's courier might have been robbed and killed, but this had happened at Mocklington, where Robyn had not been Robyn Skyrme, but Richard Eccles, and had kept himself to himself, though things had got easier after a week or two. Why had this man accosted Hendryk at all? He had only to open the letter and he would know whither they were bound after they had left Mocklington, and perhaps after that, and after that again. And though so desperate a crew might burn ricks at Unthank, at their own doors they would be as likely as not to keep up this figment of a good name, and keep the bloody-handed among them out of sight, putting forward the fairer-seeming sort, with fur caps and a civil address, who were obliging about strangers' letters and perhaps knew what was written in the twenty-second chapter of Exodus.

So Robyn was angry with Hendryk for his easy, hail-fellow ways, for if it was he himself who was the marked man, and his comings and goings *were* known, was he very much safer in one place than in another?

But the life about him was too new and exciting for such moods to last long. The snow melted, the ermined minster put on its grey lace again, and York was no longer like Unthank, all white above and dark below. Over the castle only one traitor continued to wear his shred of a night-cap long after the others were no more than poppyheads on their spikes again, and with the approach of the milder weather there were signs that Hendryk was becoming restless again, for once more he was writing his letters. But these now went with the Minster letters, and he would have been a bold robber who had tampered with those. Moreover, Hendryk now had Robyn to think of. Robyn had never seen Utrecht or Louvain or Nuremberg or Chartres, but York was as proud as the proudest of them, and it was in York that Robyn's time must be served. He was now five foot ten high, which was as tall as he would probably ever grow. His blue eyes were not those of a hind or chawbacon, vacant as the sky, but beginning to be a little drawn down at the corners, and alive with a life of their own. They were the eyes of a watcher of things, who turned them over in his mind afterwards, to find out why each was simply itself and not for a moment to be mistaken for anything else. He was full of questions too, that Hendryk was not always able to answer, for he asked him one day why it was that some crucifixes looked as if they were just about to descend into the grave, while others seemed to be just that moment rising from it. Another time he wanted to know why there were as many imps among the carvings as there were angels, and Hendryk could not tell him that either. And in York there were shops where they sold books, and Robyn was not drawing wages yet, but you might go in and read quietly without buying, and he was often to be found there when he ought to have been attending to other things.

Yet more and more it was the other things that occupied his thoughts. When this or that was to copy or replace the men often went across to the minster itself, taking with them plaster and the material for piece-moulds, and in the plaster-room adjoining the shed these replicas stood on shelves or lay stacked higgledy-piggledy on the floor, old and new together, taken yesterday or thick with years of dust, foliage and grotesques, masks that were likenesses or plain ornament just as you chose to look at them, crane-necked gargoyles, bossy crockets, string-courses and finials, and always, always the angels and the imps. Robyn made drawings of them, over which Hendryk rubbed his nose but said little, and if, as the spring came and the weather grew warm, he told Hendryk that he wanted to go out into the lanes and coppices and see the lizards darting among the stones, or the hedgehogs unrolling themselves to have a look at the world with their small bright eyes, Hendryk often let him go. But for the most part he kept him diligently at work, saying nothing about his own restlessness but sacrificing himself, which for a spirit so intractable was a very great deal. And so passed the whole of that summer and autumn, with a mild and open winter to follow, and it was in York, at a small buttery to which few but masons and stone-cutters and the cathedral men ever went, that Robyn celebrated his nineteenth birthday.

15

HE was nineteen and a half, when the chance came that neither he nor Hendryk need think twice over. His hands were deep in a great jar of soft soap that morning, for a block of stone the size of a haycock was to be got into the shed and moved accurately to a given spot, and the usual way of doing this was to jack up a plankway for it, carefully checking every inch of its slope by the spirit-level, to set it going on the slippery boards, and to see that it came to rest where it was wanted without having wrecked anything on its ponderous way. The last time Robyn had used soap except to wash himself was when he had helped the girls with Margaret Skyrme's bed-ticking, but now, with the slimy stuff smeared half-way to his elbows, he had a wager with Mechlin Tom, had made his chalk-mark, and a couple of men were starting the block on its short journey from the stone-truck and through the doorway. The soaped planks cracked and splintered; like a ram the great mass bore down and then began to ease itself off again; and Robyn flung up his arm in triumph as it came to rest flush with his chalk-mark.

'Good for you, Robyn! You'll make a mason yet!' Mechlin Tom cried, as pleased as if he had won a bet instead of losing one, and at that moment Hendryk Maas's ungainly figure obscured the doorway.

Or rather it lighted it up, for his face shone like a sun and under his spoonbill nose his mouth was stretched from ear to ear. He walked along the shed to his own working-table beyond the screen, where Robyn saw him reading a letter; but his news was too momentous to keep longer to himself, for he raised his voice.

'Hi! You, Stonecutter Skyrme or whatever you think yourself! I want you!'

'What is it?' Robyn asked, running up, for he had not seen Hendryk so radiant since that first morning of their arrival in York, now getting on for two years ago.

'You and your Pomfret Castles! The Guild men and their robes and gold chains! It's time to send for them when there's no Hendryk Maas to be had!'

'What is it? Does somebody want you to build a brace of cathedrals?'

'A brace of cathedrals! Look at this!'

'My hands are all soapy — '

'Pomfret Castle! Read it!'

But as Robyn's hands were in no state to touch the letter, he told him instead.

'They don't call it a castle, but I've seen castles you could put inside it! A Park they call it, and it has its own chapel at one end of it, with an outside pulpit to preach to them on the lawns and I don't know what! As long as we keep to the style we can do anything we like, and from the look of this it might be a couple of years' work, and it's *me* they send for, not that Guild lot with their banketting-halls and worshipful masters!'

'What, do you mean we're leaving York?' and at that Hendryk became a little less headlong.

'Nay, lad, that's leaping too far ahead. I shall have to see it first. But if it's anything like the letter says it's a job to travel across the seas for. It isn't just the pulpit, it's the chapel and all the lot, and no deans and chapters to say do this and do that, but all as *we* please! So I shall have to leave you here for a few days, because I'm doing nothing with my eyes shut. What do you think of *that*, young Robyn Skyrme, that's by way of being a mason?'

And as Hendryk got into his best clothes the very next day, and said it might be four or five days before he was back, Robyn could hardly contain himself during the full week he was away.

Maske Park was some thirty or more miles away, north of the abbey-lands, north of the great rolling Wolds too, but before the heather began that in some places might take a man a couple of days to cross. The new Lord Maske owned it, as thereabouts he owned everything else that lay between the ploughing and the grouse. Easby he owned, and Wrathby, and Kirkby Burton and Kirkby Ash, their livings and benefices and five or nine manors, and it was hardly to be supposed that Hendryk Maas should deal directly with one placed so high among the highest of all. But the Maske fires were kept ready to light year in and year out whether he was there or not, Colonel Firminger, his friend and steward, was a man of family too, and it was Colonel Firminger who had written Hendryk the letter. At the end of the week he returned, and began to get his belongings together as if he would have left again that very night.

'I cannot begin to tell you the half of it, Robyn,' he said that evening in their inn, more earnestly than Robyn had ever heard him speak before. 'But first of all I'm going to have a serious word with you. I'm not going to tell you you're a gifted lad, because you know it, sometimes a bit too well. This year and more at York's been a grand chance for you, and another couple of years here 'ld have done you no harm, even if I'd gone away myself and left you here. But at York everything takes time, for they go a lot by age. It would have been years before any higher than a foreman had as much as spoken to you. But now I'm offered this. That chapel I told you about, half of it's down on the ground. No, it isn't kings and queens this time, but just plain decay and neglect, but they say new brooms sweep clean, and Colonel Firminger or Lord Maske himself, if I do the sweeping I do it my own way. There's a roof-ridge there, that's to say, half a one. It had animals straddled along the top of it, twelve foot apart it may be. A great turtle's one, and a sea-lion's another – that was in the old admiral's day – and I've noticed the taste you have for animals and such-like. If you can make drawings that'll suit me – but that's looking ahead. You'd have been an old man before you got a chance like that at York, and all I'm saying is, I don't hold with young men being tied to old men's ideas. But mark you, young Robyn, you'd have to please *me*. If I put you on the small before the big, my word's your law. Else I'll turn you off, like any other. That's got to be settled in your head before we start.'

But already it had taken such possession of Robyn's head that he hardly closed his eyes that night.

It was on a June morning that they set out, this time with extra purchases on their cart, for things would be required that only York could furnish and Robyn was to set up with an outfit too. With the cart to push they would have to spend a night on the way, and for the first day they travelled in their working clothes; but the second day would be no more than a short stage, and if needs be they could change into something seemlier when Maske hove in sight. And because they were so many miles nearer to Sim Dacre's country it was fitting that Robyn should sing one of Sim's songs as they went:

'*As me and my marrow was gannin' to wark*
We met with the devil, it was in the dark —

'– that's you and me that's the marrows gannin' to wark, Hendryk –

'*So follow the horses, Johnny my boy.*
Follow the horses, follow 'em home.

'And I've never seen a sea-lion, Hendryk. How am I going to carve a sea-lion if I've never seen one?'

'You've never seen a mermaid, and I only said a sea-lion

used to be there,' Hendryk told him. 'There's a great library in the house, full of all manner of things, sea-lions, too, for all I know. How you do your work's *your* job.'

'What, are we to be allowed to go into the library too?'

'For sure we are, or anywhere our business takes us,' Hendryk replied, but already Robyn had broken into another song.

They slept that night at the best inn in Kirkby Burton, for Hendryk had a pocketful of wages and now Robyn was to have a small wage too. And at Kirkby Burton they were three parts there; so Hendryk did not rise very early the next morning, and took his time over his toilet, so that Robyn, too, might as well get into his best things while he was about it. For the greater state, Hendryk even talked about hiring a lad if they met one on the road, to push their cart for them, but nothing came of this, and it was towards seven o'clock of a noble June evening when Maske Park came in sight, dry-moated, with getting on for a mile of beech-hedge on the other side of the moat, and the ruddy twisted chimneys of the great mansion suddenly boring like clusters of augers up into the apricot sky. Where a bridge crossed the moat were scrolled iron gates and a lodge, but there was a smaller gate at the side, and their arrival was expected, for here a servant took charge of the cart. Half a mile ahead the house showed, a pile of brick gables and stone mullions that made Robyn catch his breath, and the great courtyard where the drive ended was surrounded on all its four sides by low latticed windows. Here they were received by a middle-aged housekeeper, the sober oval of whose hood gave her a stately and abbess-like look. She led them along a low-beamed passage to one of these courtyard chambers, where against a decorated fire-back logs crackled on the hearth, for even of a June evening a fire is a friendly greeting. A small table by the lattice was set for two, and Hendryk rubbed his hands.

'Do you mind a piece in your Bible about the salt of the earth, Robyn?' he chuckled. 'That's you and me. You can always tell the real blood-royal by the way it treats its artists. It was King Harry said he could make a hundred lords but he couldn't make a Holbein, so when you see Colonel Firminger, mind you hold your head up! We can do without them, but they can't do without us!'

'Isn't that the way the Guilds talk?' Robyn asked, but Hendryk was in one of his great moods, and passed over the pertness.

'Maybe it is, but when they get a touch of the true gold they have to hide it away, for they have their own pinchbeck to hawk,' and by the time they had washed their hands in their bedroom, which was immediately overhead, their supper was ready. They went to bed early, and the next morning there began for Robyn a life so different from anything he had ever known that he hardly knew which was the dream, his new surroundings or the world he had left behind.

Hendryk, given a free hand, had set certain men from Easby to work before returning to York to fetch Robyn, and a preliminary clearance of the chapel had already begun. As they issued from the courtyard the next morning they found the Park a shimmer of sunny mists, with dew that drenched their ankles as they made their way past the domestic buildings to the chapel at the eastern end of the house. The outside pulpit had been a graceful half-octagon of finely-fretted stone, jutting out from the chapel's south side; but ivy had forced its stones apart, tufts of wallflower had lodged in its crannies, and on the grass at its base were stacked not only its own fallen stonework, but also the larger fragments that had been carried out from the chapel itself. The round head of the sea-lion from the collapsed roof-ridge rested against the floor-slab it had broken in its descent, and next to it was a quarter of the turtle Hendryk had spoken of, with its flipper still joined on to it. Hendryk hummed and ha-ed and rubbed his nose, and then, passing in by a low undamaged archway, pointed out to Robyn the cause of half the trouble. The ends of the hammer-roofing, celery-fluted oak carved with angel's heads, had rotted on the supporting corbels, and with the giving way of one of these the rest too had been dislodged. Half the timbering lay in such disorder that it could not be examined without creeping under it. It had brought down the slating too, but the workmen had left a ladder, up which Robyn had climbed in a twink. Already he regarded that roof-ridge as his own, promised him by Hendryk if his drawings satisfied him, and on what remained of it, perched there aloft, he sat astride of a stone dolphin, gazing out over the wide lawns, the morning steaming of the grass, and the ha-ha a quarter of a mile away, beyond which cattle grazed. Looking the other way he saw the thread-like line of the distant moors, neither earth nor sky yet, and Hendryk had followed him up the ladder, and with one foot braced against a ledging of gutter was grinning at him.

'There should be trout in the streams hereabouts,' he remarked.

'I saw them feeding last night,' said Robyn.

'And past where you see all those cows, there's deer.'

'Do they hawk here? I saw some old jesses hanging in the passage.'

'I cannot tell you whether they hawk now. There's not a doubt they did.'

'And where's this library you spoke of?'

'That's right away over yonder, along a gallery, but there's a door to it from the courtyard too.'

'What's Colonel Firminger like?'

'Like?' said Hendryk, scratching his nose as he wondered how to describe Colonel Firminger without being smartly told that that wasn't him but his clothes. 'Hm. I'm not always quite sure what my own religion is, Robyn. Whiles it seems to be Early Perpendicular, but there's times it slips off into Flamboyant. But I'll say this for Colonel Firminger, if he's smashed up churches he knows where to come when he wants 'em built again, and that's good enough for you and me.'

'I wonder what there is for breakfast.'

'That's easy found out,' said Hendryk, and down from their roof and in they went to see.

Colonel Firminger, who entered the chapel that morning while Hendryk and Robyn were still considering where to begin, had very little the look of a soldier. He was a smallish, studious-looking man of fifty, soberly dressed in a coat of mole-coloured velvet, with plain instead of laced pocket-flaps. He wore his own hair, which was scanty, and carried a long paper roll instead of a sword. But for all his quiet voice Robyn was quick to notice that Hendryk used no familiarities with him, and the roll of drawings he carried was unfolded there and then.

'Make what use of them you please – or none,' he said. 'I found them in the library the day after you had left. They show the chapel as it was fifty years ago,' and after some discussion of the drawings Hendryk ventured to put in a word.

'I was about to mention the library, sir. This pupil of mine – as I explained, he was trained in York – he works under my eye – it might be convenient — '

'If he had access to the library? By all means. If he works there at nights, however, the light will be placed and taken away again by the servants. I must observe all precautions. And these beams. Can any of them be used again, or will new timber have to be estimated for?'

'It is what I am considering, sir. We shall see them better when they are stacked outside,' and after further talk Colonel Firminger inclined his head and walked away.

A week later the chapel was a half-roofed, empty shell.

The beams were laid along the walls outside with the broken stones, the debris was carried away in carts by the men from Easby. Under Hendryk's direction the poles and staging were set up, and work on the restoration of the chapel began.

16

ROBYN knew by this time why Hendryk took so little trouble to drop his voice in churches and all but whistled as he strode over their tombstone flags. His religion was also his trade, and as for sanctified places, he found no more sanctity in their fabric than he had already compassed in his own craftsman's head. All day long four building-masons from the village were busy in the chapel; foremen from the quarries came and went, the timbermen deposited their loads from the carts; but into their latticed room in the house trestles and boards were carried to make a drawing-table, for the multitude of drawings Hendryk considered it necessary to make almost passed counting. If all this (Robyn wondered) went to the restoration of one small private chapel, what miracles of labour and organization must a cathedral take? But he now began to spend his days among miracles. No sooner did one cease to astonish than another took its place. Did he weary of helping the masons in the chapel? There was the drawing-board in the house. Did a summer downpour drive the masons to shelter? There was the long walk to the library, inside by galleries and stair-heads, outside a furlong round that end of the house, with his head huddled under his coat. Did he tire even of the library, with its deep-embrasured diamond windows, its bays and shelving almost up to its moulded ceiling, its frowning mass of books old and new? By that time it had stopped raining, and there were the lawns and ha-ha, the grazing and the deer-park and the woodlands beyond. Of all this he had the freedom of his eyes and thoughts, even if only certain portions of it were his to walk in, for where the western end of the house began was a closed region on which he must not trespass.

And widest liberty of all, he, Robyn Skyrme, brought up among hinds and cheese-wenches, who had taught himself to carve an old holly-root into the shape of a pistol, might now carve anything that breathed or grew out of the earth, or if it pleased him some angel or grotesque that had never existed at all, for provided he satisfied Hendryk there was his roof-ridge to come, and anything he placed there would be signed with his own name, as he had carved the R.S. on his Unthank candlestick.

Often he fell into a musing over this new and boundless freedom. It could only be that he had been singled out for it. It was the past that had been the humdrum accident, not these shining promises ahead, for so his father, too, had been singled out before him, and had run away to sea, and disputed with learned clerks and divines – had been a soldier and fought at Pomfret siege, and had married a lady as dainty as ever rode in a coach or allowed a rough farmer to kiss her hand as she had sipped her cordial among the cushions —

So, at the appointed time and in the appointed place, the next drew invisibly nearer of itself.

That afternoon was as fiercely hot as if every veil had been withdrawn between the sun-smitten earth and the orb that rained down its leaden heat from above. The cattle had taken shelter in the ha-ha, the masons slept in the shade of the chapel walls. Robyn himself, blinded by the whiteness of new stone, had sought the library by the courtyard's shade, where he had sunk into his own chair, for the library was on the north side of the house that the sun did not reach, and with his pencils and notebooks and compasses and inks he had appropriated one of its embrasures to himself. On such a day it was difficult to keep awake, and he was not sure that he did keep awake, but if he dreamed it was such a dream as had never visited him before. Without a sound the low door at the farther end of the library opened. In the course of his trade Robyn now did a good deal of ascending and descending of ladders, as the angels in Jacob's dream had ascended and descended when he had lain with his head upon a stone, and the Unthank Bible did not say whether the angels had seen Jacob, but the girl who now entered the library certainly did not see Robyn. Noiselessly she advanced to a shelf and from it took down a large calf-bound volume. Instead of opening this, however, she placed it on the floor, leaning it against the lower books, and again thrust her hand into the opening it had left. From this she took a smaller book, which she stood reading for a moment. Then, still reading it, she walked slowly out again by the way she had come.

But there was this difference between Robyn and Jacob. Jacob had never seen the angels before, but Robyn had seen his angel before. She must be now a full seven years older, and had long outgrown that mantua that had reached down to her child's toes. No little green glove made her hand like a lord-and-lady sheath, and her coif too had gone. But the crinklets of her golden head were the same, as was the way she carried it, which Robyn could now see wide awake and plain, for the ringlets came only a little way down her neck, and her bodice sat so simply and naturally on her half-bared shoulders that in a flash he knew that Maske must be her home. She had been there all the time, yet somehow this was the first time he had seen her.

So, as if the air itself had suddenly taken shape and movement and life, she came in and went out again that afternoon, and seven years became a moment, but for Robyn that moment was the centre of time itself.

The light still lingered outside that evening, but the drawing-table in the latticed room downstairs ran along an inner wall, and Hendryk had lighted two candles the better to study Colonel Firminger's plans of the chapel as it had been fifty years ago. Robyn, half hidden in a tall chair and gazing at the unlighted fire, was casting about for how he was to find out from Hendryk what he wanted to know without letting Hendryk see the trap he was setting for him. He knew that Hendryk was the least suspicious of men, but he must not forget that on their very first meeting he had looked hard at Robyn, and asked him abruptly whether he had run away from home, and Robyn's first care now must be not to betray himself. As it chanced, however, Hendryk himself was the first to speak.

'I told the men this afternoon they could knock off for an hour. Then I went to sleep myself. What did you do?'

'Went up into the library,' said Robyn, suddenly as taciturn as a moment before he had been bursting with his question.

'Have you found your sea-lion yet?'

'No,' said Robyn, and Hendryk put Colonel Firminger's papers aside, got out others, and prepared to draw. For a quarter of an hour there was silence except for Hendryk's mutterings to himself, for he often talked to his work as if it was as good a companion as any other, and next time it was Robyn who spoke.

'Is Colonel Firminger married?' he asked.

'So *here* you go, not *there*, and be hanged to the Guilds,' Hendryk mumbled to himself as he drew. . . . 'What did you say, Robyn?'

'I asked you if Colonel Firminger was married.'

'A widower by all accounts. But I cannot give men hours off like this on another man's money. I'll have an awning rigged up to-morrow so they can work in the shade. Have you thought any more about that roof-ridge?'

'No. I don't mean I haven't been thinking about it, but

those big blocks frighten me. I'd like to start on something smaller, a capital or something. Which side was Colonel Firminger in in the troubles?'

'There's no two guesses about that. But it's because first one side wins and then the other that the likes of us have chapels to do.'

'Does he live here when Lord Maske comes to stay?' and at that Hendryk looked round over his shoulder.

'Here's a sight of questions about Colonel Firminger! What's it to you whether he's a widower or not and which side he was on in the troubles? He knows what's due to artists and their calling, which is more than you can say for some deans and chapters. But I should like you to be thinking about that roof, if it's only a small-scale to keep your mind on it. Well begun's half done, even if it's only a sketch,' and he humped himself over his drawing-board again.

To all appearances Robyn took Hendryk's advice. The next morning, in his working clothes but with his plume of hair sleekly brushed up in front, he was astride of his dolphin, where the roof of the chapel made its broken crest-combing against the sky. He was scanning the lawns and pasture beyond the ha-ha, but alas, shut off from everything else by the blank gable behind him. No distant figure appeared, reading as it walked, and he was afraid to question Hendryk further.

There were, however, other ways of finding out what he now burned to know, for the abbess-like housekeeper whose face looked out of the oval of her hood was in her turn curious about these two working-men who seemed to be on such a different footing from the builders and masons who arrived from Easby village each morning, clinked and trowelled all day, and returned to Easby again each evening. Few women found Hendryk prepossessing, but Robyn was both strong and comely, rustic it might be, but in a pastoral sort of way of his own, and he treated Mistress Eleanor with shy deference. So as she wanted to talk as much as Robyn was eager to listen all he had to do was to keep his ears open. Colonel Firminger, he learned, had taken charge at Maske when the new Lord had succeeded to the earldom. He was a widower, and before that he had moved much from place to place as some kind of Commissioner, appointed to deal with sequestrated estates and broken successions, which, Robyn reflected, might account for his having had business in the Mixton neighbourhood seven years before. Miss Betty, more properly Miss Elizabeth, had always travelled with him, moving from house to house and estate to estate while he delved into his titles and claims and inventories and what-not, always suitably entertained, as Robyn and Hendryk were entertained at Maske now; and as he and Lord Maske's father had fought together, now that things were settling down again it was likely he would remain where he was.

'You'd hardly know they were in the house,' Robyn ventured to say, and Mistress Eleanor shook herself and her bunch of keys.

'Wouldn't you, marry!' she exclaimed. 'You might think so in the chapel, that being at the east end of the house, and their apartments being in the west wing. They have their private garden there, sunk down some stone steps and all box-hedged; and Miss Betty has her own arbour, where she sits half the day in weather like this.'

'I'd rather have something to do than just sit in an arbour all day doing nothing,' said artful Robyn, and Mistress Eleanor gave a short laugh.

'Nothing to do, Miss Betty? Why, the days aren't long enough for her! She has the Colonel's papers to copy, and her music and her needlework and all the other things gentlewomen do, and nobody but her's allowed to touch her end of the garden, and she's always bringing things into the house, fledgelings that have fallen out of their nests or some animal that's hurt itself, and nursing them with milk and then letting them go again! Nothing to do, Miss Betty!'

The long and the short of all this was that Robyn, in the shade of the awning that had been rigged up in the chapel against the sun, pretended (when Hendryk's eye was on him) to be absorbed in a small model he was making of the roof-ridge in wood and wax. But more often than not he was lost in a daydream, of that box-sheltered arbour far away at the other end of the house, where Miss Betty sat playing some instrument perhaps, or reading the book she had taken from behind the other books on the library shelves, or nursing some winged thing and putting a splint on its injured twig of a leg. But Hendryk was not to be hoodwinked, and again he spoke to him as seriously as when he had told him that another year or so at York Minster would have done him no harm.

'You're beginning to get idle, Master Robyn,' he told him roundly. 'I'm an easy master as long as you make yourself a strict one, but you're not standing by the good reports I've given of you. I've seen you do more work in a day in York than you've done this last sennight here,' and Robyn answered rebelliously.

'How do you know when I'm working? You say yourself it's all inside you, and how do you know what's going on inside me?' But at that Hendryk, too, showed temper.

'It's true I don't know what's going on inside you, but I know what isn't coming out, barring that fine new lovelock that looks as if you'd been oiling it. Why have you got your best jacket on to-day? It isn't Sunday.'

'I don't keep it on when I'm working on stone.'

'And where have you been working these last two days? In the library?'

'Some of the time. Both you and the Colonel said I could.'

'Yes, and yesterday I happened to go up and see the

Colonel. I looked out of his window. What were you doing over by that hedge where those steps go down?'

'I wasn't near the steps.'

'But you were where you've no business to be. Your business is here in the chapel, and maybe in the library once in a while. If there are any errands to do at that end I'll do them.'

Alarm filled Robyn's breast, for he knew very well that he had had no business at the other end of the house. Had Colonel Firminger too seen him from the window, and said something to Hendryk about it, and was this his warning that such a thing had better not happen again? But he hadn't really been at the hedgeside. He had merely strolled along the lawns, perhaps a little further than he had been before, but nothing to make all this to-do about, and suddenly he wished he had not to share a bedroom with Hendryk, for nobody else ought to be in the same room with Robyn and his thoughts. They weren't Hendryk's thoughts, so why was he thrusting his great nose into things that Robyn himself hardly dared to peep at? But worse was to come, for after a few moments Hendryk looked sorrowfully up.

'I'm warning you not to make a fool of yourself, Robyn,' he said, in a tone that made Robyn suddenly flush crimson, and went out with his head down.

After that it was three whole days before Robyn and Hendryk exchanged another word. Robyn, flushed and angered to bursting-point, regretted that day in Umpleby's gaunt church where he had first taken up with him. Even then he had bluntly asked him whether he had run away from home; now he had spied on him from a window, and kept things back from him, for he at least had known all the time that there was a Miss Elizabeth in the house, and must have been concealing his knowledge of set purpose. What his purpose was, now that he had as much as called Robyn a fool to his face, Robyn neither knew nor cared. He and his potato of a nose came and went freely, his business with her father as his excuse; but because Robyn set his foot on a lawn down came all this on his head. Hendryk hadn't called him a fool when at a glance he had seen in him a young man of exceptional parts, and had made much of him so that nobody else should get him, and had suggested that they should throw in their lots together. Robyn didn't deny that he was a fine craftsman, with a knack of impressing himself on the church authorities; but he had a braggart's opinion of himself, and flung away money on his cordials and mixtures, and then borrowed four shillings from Robyn. He wished he had had Mechlin Tom to talk to. Tom at least didn't set himself above the Guilds and everybody the way Hendryk did —

And all this raging was simply because for seven long years something he had hardly known he had harboured had been quietly growing in his breast, winding itself into him as a tree's roots lock themselves about a stone. He remembered his parentage and threw up his lovelocked head. Did such a man as his father, a dainty little rose-diamond like his mother, beget a nobody for their son? But here his indignation trembled and broke. If some artist had painted that bright little miniature of his mother, even then heavy with himself, and her eyes full of a thousand dreamy thoughts, he would have admired his craft and skill; but rough John Skyrme had practised no art in his telling of it. They had emerged of themselves, those curls like a golden waterdog's, and of themselves they had become one with those other curls and their coif and netting of gold, of the child setting foot in her chair as she had issued from Mixton church porch. Apart, yet year by year with himself, she had grown up, that was all. Nay, she was still growing, for while those few moments in the library had shown him only her head bent over the book and the house-like simplicity of her uncovered shoulders, the rest now added itself – the little points of her sleeves that Mistress Eleanor or some tire-woman would have to tie about her arms for her, prinking and puffing them daintily out, the little bodice with its lappets behind her waist, the gathering of the falling petticoats with her own young life hidden under their folds, an apricock-bud newly burst.

And Hendryk, seeing her father, must on occasion see her too; and up boiled his anger afresh. He didn't care if Hendryk did think him a fool. After that it would be Hendryk Maas the master, not Robyn Skyrme the pupil, who would have to speak the first.

And so it was, for on the third evening Hendryk appeared in their parlour doorway, jàcketed, his broad hat on his head and the dust of the day's work brushed from his shoes. 'What say you to a walk, Robyn?' he said, in a tone as even as if nothing had happened, and for a moment Robyn wondered whether he had at last seen the injustice of it all, and meant a stroll over the lawns, as far as the other end of the ha-ha perhaps, where the western portion of the house could be seen, and he rose and pushed back his lovelock of hair.

But instead Hendryk took him quite the other way. He took him, not towards the front of the house, but to the back, and out by a postern, where the ground rose to a plantation. But at one point a clearing had been made, from which they could see the great place, as it lay below them, its auger-like clusters of brick chimneys, its vanes and stepped gables and outbuildings, even their own latticed window, together with the other windows of that side of the courtyard. And here Hendryk stopped, and put an arm round Robyn's shoulder, and turned him so that he might see it all too, and spoke to him in a voice he had never used to him before.

'Just look at it, Robyn,' he said as if he could hardly trust himself to speak. 'Just look at it, and then tell me if there's any more to be said.'

Robyn looked, and gulped, but did not reply, and Hendryk went on.

'Don't say anything till you've thought a minute. I know well it isn't Colonel Firminger's, and I don't want you to answer me as you answer me sometimes about things that don't matter a deal, that it belongs to Lord Maske, and the Colonel's only his steward, and ill-thought things like that. Colonel Firminger's held the King's Commission as a soldier. He's been a Commissioner of Lands too, and those are offices they're picked and chosen for, not the first that comes along. It's another world, Robyn, and each to his world is the way things are, ay, the Guilds too if it comes to that, for I know my bark's often worse than my bite, but it eases me, and there's times the quintain swings round and catches me a clout too. Are you following me?'

'Yes,' said Robyn, again looking down on the assemblage of roofs.

'You and me's seen a few places together now. We've seen churches, flagged all over their floors and walls with all that's left of great lords and ladies and their like, like that Robertus you couldn't spell out because it was in Latin. Always the world's coming to a stop without 'em, but what happens when they're dead? It's then they send for you and me. The sexton can bury 'em, Robyn, but it's when he's finished *we* begin. I don't want to tell you more than's good for you, but fame would be a fickle thing without a few remembrancers like us, and little enough to make it out of sometimes. So if we can do that, isn't ours a life worth having, too?'

Still Robyn was unable to reply for the gulping in his throat.

'I say it is, Robyn, but we have to give ourselves to it. Better give nothing than give half of yourself. Life's a struggle, as you know by now, but it's inside you the hardest of the struggle is. It isn't thinking how grand it would be to be grand, but sticking to your trade that's got to keep you in heart. Whatever ails the rest of you, nothing must happen to that. Do you take me?'

'I know what you mean,' said Robyn in a low voice.

'Then what about making a fresh start to-morrow? I know what you mean about feeling your roof-ridge perhaps a bit beyond you, so try something easier. There's ten new capitals to design, with frogs and field-mice for all I care, not to speak of the running leafwork and the corbel-ends and an odd saint or two for the pulpit. Try wood for a change. But mark this: if you find your thoughts running away with you, that's when a man has to work till he falls asleep on his feet. So what say you, lad?'

So according to Hendryk, Robyn might do one thing or the other, but not both; and as he stood looking down on the house the sinking sun turned its chimney-stacks to sentinels taking over their duties for the night, and the lower sky sombred to dusky fruit-like browns, and the courtyard below was lost in shadow. Far away to the south the last of the day died on the hummock of the Wolds, and the brighter for the darkness of the plantation the evening star hung in the sky like a silver pellet. Robyn stood looking at it. He had seen it a thousand times before, but never before so patient-looking and steadfast and clear.

But suddenly he dropped his eyes again, for another light had gone up. And this was a light he had not seen before, for never before had he been in the plantation at that hour. It came from an upper window of the western end of the house.

17

WHAT did it now profit Robyn Skyrme that Nature had cast him in the artist-mould? According to Hendryk it was to possess the key of another and a boundless world, but to

Robyn it was to be denied something that even the lowliest possessed. Even Hendryk had to put something in its place, something that came out of a jar or bottle, and why was he always so careful to remove the traces of it whenever he put on his jacket to see Colonel Firminger? But Robyn's own breath was as sweet as that of an animal that lives on herbage. If sometimes his eyes were rimmed it was with inner trouble, not with that that drowns trouble, and his thoughts were as little tainted. So – ladies on their flat stone tables, placidly sleeping with their garters on their arms and their heads on their cold cushions and their small feet and hands alike pointed upward in prayer? Somewhere under this same roof there was a pair of gently-sloping shoulders, and sleeve-points that had to be tied for her, and ringlets that twinkled on her head in little flickers of gold. Only a corridor or two away, only a few chambers away, there she was, busy all day with her gentle little occupations or helping her father with his writing, and yet it might as well have been so many leagues! He tried to guess what her book had been. In Mixton church-porch it had been a psalter, and she had carried it in her muff, but here she kept it behind a tall folio, and be sure he had looked behind that folio too, but had found nothing, and had put it back again with an odd feeling of shame. But at least his hand as well as her own had rested on that folio.

Outside the house he had been chidden for trespassing beyond the lawns. Inside it the library was as far as he was licensed to go. But now there were ten new capitals to design, and having said what he had to say, Hendryk said no more. So be it. If he was a fool he was a fool, so what then? In the library Robyn and his materials for drawing were more and more frequently to be found.

The inside way to the library, that by the long windowed gallery that looked down on the courtyard, was far from being all on one level. Here a couple of steps downward might break it, rising again a yard or two further on, and there were two staircase-heads, with small landings, one at the eastern end and the other where the staircase rose from the courtyard direct. But the light from the courtyard windows was passed on to the library itself by a kind of inner clere-story, too high to be looked over, and beyond the second staircase an abrupt angle closed the view.

It was towards this angle that Robyn always stood gazing for a few moments before he pressed the hasp of the library's second door. This was not his proper way, for the first door would have been the whole length of the library nearer, but if Mistress Eleanor or anybody happened to surprise him he could always pretend that something down in the courtyard had caught his attention and that he had walked on with-out noticing, and it was beyond that shallow well of two steps that she must have appeared on that torrid afternoon when she too had come for her book. And if some volume with a sea-horse in it happened to be at that end of the great book-lined chamber it was really no further outside than in.

He had just reached this second door one afternoon when he thought he heard a step beyond the angle. Wishing with all his heart that he had taken the nearer way he stood there like a thief caught in the act. But the figure that turned the corner, dropped the two steps into the well and then reached the level again, was not the figure of his dreams. It was the quiet, mole-coloured figure of Colonel Firminger.

His heart was in his mouth. For all he knew the Colonel had already seen him from the western window on that after-noon when he had trespassed beyond the lawns as far as the box-hedge, and now he was caught entering the library by a roundabout way. With his eyes on the ground the Colonel continued to advance, and suddenly he found the library door standing open for him. Robyn, as flat as a board against the wainscot, was making way for him to enter first.

At that the Colonel lifted his eyes. He saw Master Robyn, brushed and combed and necklothed, carrying papers and a pair of compasses, and it was on these that his eyes rested first.

Then he looked up into the lad's glowing face.

'Ah, yes. You are the pupil from York,' and Robyn saw that he too carried a large book.

'Yes, sir,' Robyn stammered.

'I was told you worked in the library. I have not come to disturb you. I only came to replace this book. Pray enter,' and passing in himself he made way for Robyn. 'One moment. There was something I had on my mind. Ah, yes. Do you work up here at night?'

'No, sir.'

'It was only about the lights. Have what lights you need, but be so good as to ask for them and leave them burning when you have finished. I will give orders about it.'

'I had already been told, sir.'

'I do not ask what you are busy upon, for it is not to get the best out of an artist or craftsman to stand over him as he works. Anything else you may require — '

On the instant Robyn found himself playing with a hardy thought. Colonel Firminger said nothing about box-hedges, and the forbiddance might have come from Hendryk only. His work that afternoon was on one of the ten new capitals that were to replace the old, and into it he had wrought the famous squirrel wringing out its drenched tail. He was in truth a little set-up about his design, here he was, in conversation with the major-domo of the estate itself, and no Hendryk to thrust his spoke in. He took his courage in both hands.

'I'm doing one of the new capitals, sir,' he said modestly, and the Colonel gave him a mildly inquiring look.

'Ah. Not the roof-ridge? You mean it is sufficiently advanced to be seen?'

For answer Robyn led the way to the small table he had carried into the farthest embrasure from which they stood, produced his drawing, and waited. Colonel Firminger stood looking for a few moments at the squirrel. Then he did a thing that Robyn had an idea he did not do very easily – he smiled.

'This is your own work?'

'Yes, sir.'

'It is both delicate and firm. You have others?'

'Not yet worked out, sir.'

'And each capital is to be different?'

'A different subject, sir, but —,' and he fumbled for the word that should tell Colonel Firminger that the capitals should have each its sister-spirit of lightsomeness, and the Colonel smiled again.

'When you have finished for to-day I should be obliged if you would leave your squirrel here. You will find it in the same place in the morning. You will remember about the lights. I will now leave you to your work,' and Colonel Firminger crossed the library, replaced his book, and went out again by the way he had come.

Robyn's heart was heaven-high. Seeing his squirrel this quiet, elderly, rather harassed-looking gentleman-steward had smiled. That he should want to take it away, bringing it back again in the morning, could mean only one thing: he wished to show it to his daughter, who succoured the fallen fledgelings and nursed the small maimed things back to health. Even if the Colonel had not said it was a firm, delicate piece of work, he would have known this by the beating of his own heart, and that his squirrel was to be his messenger, and that Hendryk was wrong, and it was *not* one thing or the other, but there *was* a middle way.

Yet the next moment his uplifting was as if it had never been. Colonel Firminger, coming upon him at the wrong door, must inevitably have wondered why he chose the farther way round to get to his own table. If Hendryk had seen him from the western window the colonel-steward might well have seen him loitering by the box-hedge too. Hendryk wrote letters, entrusting them to the civil-spoken stranger who came along, and was perturbed that they did not come to hand; but Robyn's own fortune was no better. His squirrel was a sigh that lost itself in the air, a message without an answer, for there the next morning it was on his table again, just so many lines on a piece of paper, that for a moment had brought a smile to Colonel Firminger's close locked lips, but left Robyn as he was before. Hendryk was only too dismally right. Robyn was not even a maimed animal, to be fed for a day or two with hot milk and then to be set free again. The library itself became a cage and a place of maimed thoughts and the preciousness of longing wasted. As a record of his misery his squirrel, set up in stone, might endure for an age. As a record of anything else it could only call him what Hendryk called him – a fool.

So after another week of wasteful waiting he ceased to haunt the library. Better those other dreams, the workman dreams that come to a man who works till he falls asleep on his feet. One capital finally completed might show the way to the next, and that to the next again, till all ten were done, and so much of Robyn done too, and the chapel itself finished, after which it was in his mind to say good-bye to Hendryk and take his chance in the world alone. The prentice-way of setting about his capital would have been to begin with a clay model, but one morning found him setting up a block of stone. He pinned up his drawing under the chapel awning and assembled his drills. He had his working smock on again and his leather apron about his waist, and his cap was thrust carelessly over his plume of fair hair. Hendryk, busy outside at his pulpit, saw very well what he was doing, but let him alone. Day followed day uncounted, for only so do we break that which otherwise would break us. Robyn's mouth was firm and set as, discarding his drills, he knocked off the lumps that fell with a soft thud in the dust. Yet if you had told him that he was learning what life was made of, his answer would have been a stare.

With the change to smaller tools it was as if the stone itself began almost imperceptibly to move. Something muffled in it was calling to be let out, and it was to this that Robyn must marry himself, to the stone and its grain and nature, not to mistresses whose fathers smile but themselves remain hidden a house's length away. And on the day when his squirrel emerged there stood Hendryk too behind him, and the two of them stood looking at it together, and yet Robyn only gave himself a surly shake when Hendryk put his hand on his shoulder.

'Well done, Robyn,' he said.

'I knew you thought I was going to spoil a block of stone,' Robyn grunted, but Hendryk shook his head.

'You'll spoil lots of stone before you've finished, at least I hope you will,' he said. 'That's only half of what I meant.'

But Robyn didn't want to hear the other half of what Hendryk meant, and there was the squirrel, cunningly spied on in its foliated chamber at its own private business and ready for its tree. There, too, stood the headless shaft of the pillar, a gap, and then the spring of the arcade above it. But as Robyn carried it up the ladder to its niche, and then carried it like a ponderous baby down again to cut a deeper incision, then up and down again to do something else, he was already wondering whether the toad blinking round its burdock would work out the same. He was not elated; rather he was grimly satisfied, ready to set about the toad to-morrow, and after that the remaining capitals out of hand. But it chanced that at that moment Hendryk was called away. Robyn had set the capital on its shaft again and was standing looking up at it, the small square of looking-glass he had been using still in his hand. At that moment he heard a laugh and a whispering and a shy scuffling. He turned, and then stood stock still, for that which he had sought for so long was there of itself. With the friend who had come to Maske to visit her, she stood in the chapel doorway.

18

THEY are wrong who say that three is no company when without the third there would be no meeting. Now that Robyn came to think of it, he remembered that he had seen Colonel Firminger an hour before, riding off in the direction of Easby, but now his mind was a whirl of furtive observations and abashed avoidances. He could see that this third person was a shade taller and more mischievously dark-eyed and perhaps a year older than the one he had not looked at yet, but in the sun and shadow of the stripped chapel he could be sure of little, and if they had straightway vanished again their vanishing would have been all one with their appearance. But they did not vanish. Instead of vanishing, the other had passed her arm about the one's waist, and was looking with bold-eyed curiosity at Robyn. Then she tossed her head in her nineteen-year-old way.

'May we see the wonderful squirrel?' she said.

Robyn's cap was off, his hair tumbled sideways over his forehead. For a fleeting moment he wondered why his squirrel should be called wonderful, but the one who had spoken had the ways of one who had recently learned a fashionable air and was losing no opportunity of practising herself in it. Her eyes had followed Robyn's upwards, and Robyn, his bit of looking-glass still in his hand, looked first at her and then at the squirrel again.

'There it is,' he said.

'But we can't see it properly up there. You've only just carried it up. Please carry it down again.'

Again Robyn mounted the ladder and lifted the heavy stone from its place. He set it on his working block and stood back, but again the other was looking at him as much as at his carving, and then her eyes fell on his bit of looking-glass.

'Is that what you were flashing across the lawn like a bird-snare?' she asked. 'Did you catch your squirrel that way?'

Then Robyn caught her meaning, and flushed. She meant that he, like the squirrel, had been caught at his toilet, and if she intended it for drollery it missed its mark, for here Robyn was able to pack her off back to school again. Looking at her as straight as if she had been no more than a carving herself, he told her that work that is to be seen from below must be wrought from below, and that a piece of looking-glass that could be tilted to any angle was a necessary tool of his trade. Also, he informed her for her good, to work always in one light was to work with only half an eye, since the light changed almost as you watched it, and so your work would never be finished. He was not in the least afraid of this young madam who called his squirrel wonderful before she had seen it and thought that Robyn carried a looking-glass in his pocket to look at his own face in.

But none of this misled him for a moment. But for Miss Firminger she would never have heard of the squirrel, and Miss Firminger had not yet opened her mouth. And Miss Valentine (as he presently discovered the name of the one who did the talking to be) was looking at his working clothes, so let her look, for Robyn was proud now that he had them on, and knew that he would have looked a fool to be carrying powdery blocks of stone up and down ladders in his best jacket or pretending that his tumbled hair was damp with anything but sweat.

Then he glanced down at Miss Firminger's small feet. Though she had only advanced a few paces into the chapel they were white with dust, and as his eyes stole slowly upwards he saw that her petticoats that day were of brown satin, and stood out in little ridges as if they too had been carved with a tool, and as his eyes rose higher still he saw the satin sleeves tumbling loosely over their tagged laces, and the little white under-edging where her bodice crossed her shoulders, and a gossamer shawl to keep the sun from their whiteness. And he saw too what made her golden hair almost more gold than gold itself, for she had tied little yellow ribbons into its ringlets, and the hair and the ribbons together shone like buttercups.

But just as he was about to finish his look he found himself staring into a pair of eyes as different from Miss Firminger's as could well be imagined. Horse-like in his hinged dust-blinkers, great-nosed and shambling, Hendryk had returned and stood looking at them all three.

But Robyn had already turned away. Hendryk too was in his mason's clothes, but at the sight of his pepper-box nose Miss Valentine's manner had changed in a twink. It was not Hendryk she had come to see, and Robyn did not accompany them as they were borne abruptly off to see the pulpit outside. By that time he was up his ladder again, returning his capital to its place. And when he descended it was to sit down on his working block, to slip his looking-glass into his pocket, and to remain there, gazing down at the dust at his feet.

No need to follow Robyn Skyrme's thoughts now, for they were no longer his own. It would be easy enough to find out from Mistress Eleanor who this newly grown-up young lady was who had descended on the house, but why put himself to the trouble? It needed neither herald nor trumpet to announce *her* part in the matter. Weeks ago his squirrel had been his message. Now, at the first opportunity, Miss Valentine was the bearer of the answer to it. He had not looked into those shy eyes set round with their ringing of yellow and gold; nay, this was only the third time in all these years that he had been within speaking distance of her; but now that *she* did the speaking, though another carried the words for her, was he supposed not to hear? He glanced sideways at his squirrel on its stone tree. Though king or queen or parliament brought it tumbling down again to-morrow it had done all he asked of it and beyond price or counting more, so what after that did Hendryk and his head-shakings matter? What did his own thumping heart matter, or her unsmiling father, or anything else on the earth or beneath it? Only to tell her that he loved her, to whisper to his own heart that now she knew it, and then if needs be to go on his way – he asked no more. Not in one lifetime do such things happen twice. Stand gazing at them as they pass and it is the laggard and doubter who carries the tragedy in himself. There was no sign of them when Robyn went out, and, avoiding Hendryk, made his way to his own room. He changed into his best kerseys, not to please anybody else now but to please himself. His solitary walk that evening took him up to the plantation again, and from its clearing he paused to look down on the house. Its vastness did not overwhelm him now. If it was too great, give him only its small treasure and let the rest go. He continued his ascent through the wood, and where else he went that evening he did not know. Hendryk was waiting for him when he returned, but he went straight to bed, and when Hendryk followed him an hour later there was no conversation. He continued to lie awake long after Hendryk slept.

He would not have been Robyn, however, if he had not contrived to put himself in Mistress Eleanor's way the very next day, but what he learned only started a new flock of questions. Miss Valentine's home, it seemed, was in York, and it had taken Hendryk and himself two easy days to make the journey on foot. In her father's coach she had driven it easily within the safe hours of daylight, and the smallness of the equipage was no doubt the reason why Robyn had not heard it arrive. But she was a bird of passage only, was leaving again the next day but one, and it was this that again woke the fears in Robyn's breast. When she had gone would not things be once more exactly as they had been before? Or suppose she had come only to bear her friend off with her? For a whole day he lived in suspense, without seeing or hearing any more of either of them. At nine o'clock of the morning of the day after that he heard sounds of preparation in the stables beyond the courtyard and hurried round to see, looking from beyond a wall as at Mixton church-porch he had watched from behind the scaffolding. The coach was being got out and the horses made ready. He sped round the chapel to the outside pulpit, where he dropped on his knees for concealment, looking as if he was saying his prayers, which perhaps he was. Then his heart grew light again. The coach and its attendants advanced at a walk along the drive beyond the ha-ha, but Miss Firminger, walking slowly with Miss Valentine across the lawn, was not dressed for departure. He saw the buttercup of her head as they advanced to where the coach waited with its driver on his seat, the manservant behind and the two outriders standing by their horses. Colonel Firminger was not there. It seemed an age before the two figures embraced, the cavalcade moved away, Miss Firminger stood fluttering her handkerchief after it and then returned across the lawn, alone. Robyn rose from his knees again. His star had stood his friend. Now it was he who must follow his star.

Hendryk had begun to accept it without comment that Robyn, going to bed early, should leave him to follow when he wished. If he found him asleep, well; if the bed was empty, well again, for Robyn considered himself free to breathe the evening air for half an hour or so if he chose, and nothing had been said about lawns after sunset, when the household was within doors. Hendryk, entering the room on the night of the coach's departure, found nobody there. There was no sign of him in the courtyard, so Hendryk undressed and went to bed.

Robyn was, in fact, far away on the other side of the house, wandering alone down by the ha-ha, afraid, now the moment had come, to approach the flitting, moth-like figure, hardly to be seen against the distant box-hedge, that also was taking the air before retiring for the night.

And on the following evening Robyn was out so late that Hendryk first cursed Robyn and his star, then sighed deeply, and gave it up.

The last of the day had hardly yet gone, the new moon only just sunk out of sight. None knew better than Robyn that he too might as well have been in bed as pacing the deep ha-ha's verge and upbraiding himself for his cowardice of the night before. Indeed, his opportunity might now have gone for ever, for on the night before he had at least had that momentary glimmer. Now, though he strained his eyes, he saw nothing. Only a single window was lighted at that end of the house, which he knew to be Colonel Firminger's window. That she too might be in that same room only made the light more mocking and unapproachable.

But the next moment he *had* seen, for it is in such ways that women talk. Something in a habit of cockchafer-brown was moving furtively by the hedge. Like a dissimulating lantern that opens and closes its shutter, the shadow seemed to blink for a moment, showing some paler garment underneath. If that light in the window had been a warning light she would not have been there, so it must be a friendly light, and his courage came upon him. Her father was busy with his papers; the danger would come if the lights moved or went out; and though he had no more idea than a sleepwalker what he should say when he reached the hedge, he was already leaving a dim trail behind him in the dewy grass. Again the cockchafer-brown opened and closed for a moment, this time a little further away from the house. The next moment (though of that moment he knew nothing) he was standing by her, glancing fearfully at the light over the hedge-top, and somehow able to speak himself though her own voice was a voice he had not yet heard.

'I saw the coach go,' he said, hardly moving his lips, and instantly thought what an idiot's thing it was to have said, for all that was yesterday, and half the household had seen the coach go, though not one of them with his own dumb fear lest she should go with it. Why had he not said that he had seen her from the ha-ha *last* night timidly yet daringly letting him know that she was there, so that to-night he might please himself whether he answered her signal or not?

Then for the first time in his life he heard her voice, hurried, afraid, as if she would be glad when some foolhardy thing was over, but bravely carrying out a behest.

'I have a message to give you. She made me promise. Then I must go in.'

But the message didn't come, and he found his voice again.

'I was afraid you were going away too.'

'Come a little further away. I was to tell you she was deeply offended with you.'

Miss Valentine! Offended with him! Why? And 'Why?' he asked in astonishment.

'For not coming out with us to see the pulpit, but just sitting there on that block like a pixie on a toadstool, after she'd taken all that trouble,' and Robyn's eyes opened wide in the dusk of the box-hedge.

For what should he have known of the ways of two young women when they put their heads together, and glance at a young man, and whisper 'You!' and 'No, you!' and push one another forward. And it might be either or neither of them, but very plainly it is them both as long as they are together! Miss Valentine was the older and bolder of them, but there is never any certainty in that, and they were yards along the hedge now, and the light of the window could not be seen, and the new moon had disappeared long ago. Neither was Robyn Skyrme taking all this risk to talk about Miss Valentine.

'I saw you last night,' he said huskily. 'I was down by the ha-ha.'

'I didn't see you.'

'You walked nearly as far as this twice, and then went in.'

'She said she *knew* you would be there, and made me promise to give you her message.'

'And I've seen you before then, before I even knew who you were.'

'You've seen *me* before? Where?'

'At a place called Mixton. It was on a Sunday, and you'd been to church.'

'Mixton in Lincolnshire? But that must be years and years ago! Father was there on a Commission, and I did go to church, but I should have forgotten all about it except that it was the first time I had a chair all to myself!'

'I hadn't forgotten.'

'What, all those years ago?'

'Yes, all those years ago,' and there was an astonished silence.

And she had delivered her message from Miss Valentine, and there was nothing further for her to stay for, yet there they still stood, with the silence slowly building itself up between them like a wall again, that there would be no squirrels and saucy Miss Valentines to break down a second time. He began to mutter.

'Why did she say that?'

'Who? Say what?'

'That about my sulking like a pixie on a toadstool.'

'But those are the things she says. She's always saying things that make you laugh.'

'Who is she?'

'Celia? She's my greatest friend. We've always known one another.'

'I wanted to come with you to the pulpit, but I won't when *he*'s there.'

'Mr Maas?'

'Hendryk his name is.'

'You're his pupil, aren't you?'

'At York I was.'

'Celia lives in York,' and he was about to say yes, he knew, but she might ask him how he knew, and that would bring Mistress Eleanor in, so he mumbled something else instead, trying to see her face as he said it, but she had taken a step back to see whether the light in the window had moved yet.

'I was up in the pulpit when she went. Do you know what I was afraid of?'

'What?'

'That you might be going with her,' and it must have occurred to her that that was a shockingly forward thing for him to have said, for she huddled the dark cloak about her, casting it over her head too.

'I must go. I daren't think what Father would say if he knew.'

'Now that she's gone do you mean I shan't see you any more?' he asked in a suddenly agonized voice, and at the end of the long pause that followed her own was barely a whisper.

'I daren't come to the chapel by myself.'

'And Hendryk says I've no business at this end of the house —'

It was the wall again. She stepped back, and the next time she did not step forward, for apparently something had happened to the light. She drew in her breath, but her whole body seemed to say 'No!' as he made as if to follow her. 'Good night,' she said in quick agitation, and the next moment had gone.

One moment there, the next gone. So stupefying a difference did it make that he could only stand there, waiting and listening for sounds before casting circuitously away from the house, round by the dangerous ha-ha, and so to where he properly belonged. Hendryk was asleep when he tiptoed up to his chamber.

But he did not notice that Hendryk asleep now seemed a far, far happier man than Hendryk awake.

They say that learned men, wise in the motions of the stars, can still trace back the changes of that moon that was already setting when Robyn Skyrme met Betty Firminger that first time, in the warm blackness of the box-hedge at the western end of Maske Hall. But skilled indeed he would have to be to revive to-day its phases as they had their way in those two eager and tremulous yet so different young breasts. The month was September, no cloak needed yet against the chilling of the air, yet already a brown cockchafer cloak had become their signal, a closed lantern of a thing, with all its light inside. Even if she had not been there the next night he would still have been waiting for her, a little closer in by the hedge this time, so as not to miss the brief unfolding of those dark hawk-moth wings that revealed the lighter garment underneath and closed again while she was still yards away. But she was there, for it was now he who was all afire to hear what else Miss Valentine had to say, and the hedge, so close to the house, was a perilous place for such nocturnal adventures. On a still night the lowest murmur might carry; their single safety was that the lighted window could be seen from there; and if they stole down the three stone steps into the sunken garden with its trimmed high box all round and the dark sheltering arbour at the end they would not even have the warning of the changing light.

But if from there she heard her father call she could call back, 'Here I am, Father,' and he could slip away when all was quiet again, and however it was, on tiptoe down the three stone steps she beckoned him on the third night, and no less stealthily he followed her, to hear all about Miss Valentine, and how strange and romantic it was that she should have seen his bit of looking-glass twinkling across the lawn like a jack-o'-lantern, and straightway fallen into a love-sickness, and sent her faithful go-between with a tender reproach.

But it was not Miss Valentine who had ridden in her chair to Mixton church all those years ago, and looked, like himself, at the same tall window with its saints standing up like birds in their nests in its branching tree. Squirrels had lived in the trees long before saints had, and as their thoughts strayed away from the absent Miss Valentine, squirrels led to capitals, and capitals to the small hurt creatures she carried across to the house to nurse, and one thing to another, and so on and what you will, as long as the moon rose a little later each night, and the crest of the dark hedge above them became a roof-ridge as the thin silver spread across the sky, and suddenly its peeping tip showed her face in its corner, and her uncovered head soft as a glow-worm in its yellow ribbons, and something shy yet venturesome in her eyes that did not belong to Celia Valentine at all.

But time was slipping by, and the love of those who waste it on anything but itself quickly goes the way of the rest of the unimpetuous loves of the world. Whether she had been helping her father that day, or playing her lute or tending her garden, seemed to him of infinitely less importance than what her thoughts were now. Yet it was from these that he still drew back, grumbling about other things instead.

'I wish I had a room to myself,' he muttered that night,

trying to see her face, for the moon had not crept round yet, and as she also pouted he was quick to notice that she too had lived much in other people's houses, though never in so vast a place as this.

'Rooms! Here! Can't you tell Mistress Eleanor you want one?'

'I could have done when we first came. I daren't now.'

'She'd have to if *I* told her, but I daren't either, because father might get to hear.'

'Hush. Listen. What was that?'

They listened, but it was nothing, and he next grumbled because he couldn't see her, only the glimmer of her ribbons, and at that she changed her whisper, as if she had just thought of some tale of enchantment and awe.

'Don't you know why you can't see me?'

'No. Why?'

'I'm not here. I'm not anywhere. I've made myself invisible and vanished.'

'Your hand hasn't vanished.'

'All but my hand has.'

'It had a green glove on the first time I saw it, and what was that book you came into the library for that afternoon?'

'A book?' she said, pretending not to remember, but he could tell by the way she said it that she remembered very well.

'Yes. It was hidden behind one of the big ones, and you had to take the big one down to get it, and you took it away and didn't bring it back.'

'How do you know I didn't bring it back?'

'Because I looked,' and he did not blush as he said it now.

It was Celia's. She sent it to me by the post.'

That isn't saying what it *is*,' he said, as he had formerly said to Hendryk when he had asked him what somebody was like and Hendryk had described the man's clothes.

'Ask Celia. You can write her a letter.'

'Why had it to be hidden away like that?'

'Because I wasn't to show anybody. A Scottish gentleman called Hamilton wrote it, in French, and it's all about the Court, and some of it's very naughty. Do you know French?'

'No, so you'll have to tell me,' and suddenly he missed her hand, for she drew it away quite quickly.

'That would be a pretty thing!' she said. 'Now I *have* vanished!'

But in some mysterious way the book that the Scottish gentleman had written in French made yet another difference, and when he had found her hand again he drew it round his neck, pulling it down over his breast so that she could feel the thudding of his heart. And so far the moon was only just past its first quarter.

19

CARPENTERS were now at work in the chapel, for Hendryk had long ago decided that the details of the roofing must be carried out elsewhere, had designed corbel-ends of his own, and had sent his drawings off to York to craftsmen he could trust. Now half the roof was back again, there were new men about the place, and as they scarfed and bolted and set up their pulleys for the hoisting of the great longitudinal roof-tree there was plenty of company for Robyn to talk to. This was well, for Hendryk now spoke little, and it was sometimes Robyn himself who, out of some perverse compunction, went out of his way to talk to him as he had formerly talked. None the less, if the price of Hendryk Maas's conversation was that Robyn Skyrme should give an account of how he now spent his evenings, Hendryk must make the best of his own society, and the carpenters were after all not very amusing fellows. They measured and scarfed and set their tackle and grunted over their augers as they drilled the holes for their great bolts, but Robyn, a stone-worker, now looked down on them and their soft and womanish wood. At the proper time, when their rude labours were finished, he, Robyn the master, would begin and show them what was underneath that fair plume of hair of his. Combing the sky with their cock-crests, up would go his sea-horses and dolphins, a great turtle perhaps or perhaps a mermaid, to show Colonel Firminger and the world the sort of artist they had among them. In the meantime his capitals occupied his days. As his squirrel had taken shape, so now his toad and burdock-leaves were beginning to emerge, and if once in a while Hendryk happened to pause to see what he was doing he invented ahead work he had not yet begun.

'An owl's going to be the next,' he said one day. 'I'm going to work it in a pattern of branches, all thick and wintry with rime.'

'An owl,' Hendryk nodded. 'Then that'll be three of 'em done.'

'And after that perhaps a bat, a sort of lacing of bats. Their wings fit into that shape.'

'Show me the drawings when you've made 'em. There's ten to do.'

'Well, a bat and an owl are two, and there's one on its shaft behind you, and I shall finish this in another week – that's nearly half.'

'In the stuff thoughts are made of. Have you thought any more about the ridge?'

'The timbers aren't up yet — ' Robyn began, but checked himself, for here he saw a chance to placate Hendryk. That evening, Miss Betty Firminger had told him there would be no meeting, for her father had told her he would require her services. So, changing his mind, 'Hendryk,' he said, 'shall we start the drawings for that ridge this evening, both of us?'

And Hendryk looked hard at him through his splinter goggles.

'What, in the house?' he said.

'Yes.'

'As you like,' said Hendryk, and turned away.

That evening, in their own sitting-room, Robyn got out his materials and drew up his chair to the drawing-board. There could be no doubt Hendryk was in a huff, for no pupil can be keeping secret assignations in a sunken garden night after night and be getting on with his work at the same time. So he ostentatiously lighted his two candles, and squared himself to his plans, and hoped that Hendryk, whose nose was thrust into a book over by the hearth, would notice how industrious he was. But suddenly Hendryk, without even changing his position, spoke in a voice without any emotion whatever.

'Robyn – if I might have a word with you —'

Robyn, pencil in hand, half turned in his chair.

'I've been speaking with Mistress Eleanor to-day. I cannot have my nights broken by late comings-in the way they have been this last week and more. There's no lack of rooms in this house. There's one next to the room over our heads, or there's others. You'd better see her about it.'

'What do you mean?' Robyn demanded, but Hendryk's nose was in his book again.

'Nay, I've finished. You'll find the beds made up. Take which you like, and I'll take the other.'

Without a word Robyn pushed his work aside and went upstairs. Twenty things now made him angry. For the first time Hendryk had spoken like a man who wished to spare not Robyn, but himself. It was precisely what he had wanted but had not dared to ask for; she had dared it even less than himself; yet now that he had it he was in a sudden rage about it. Could Hendryk have found no more friendly way than this? Nay, there was not even any advantage in the new room across the passage, for both looked down on the court-yard alike and the same staircase led to them both. And it must be on this night, when he stood most in need of a kind word from a friend, that Hendryk told him he might go his own way for henceforward he washed his hands of him. Now nothing would have dragged him downstairs into the same room with Hendryk Maas again. He looked at the new bed and the moonlight that cut across a corner of the casement. That same moon would just be beginning to shine over the box-hedge, and she was closeted with her father, the head with the buttercup ribbons bent over his dull working-books and accounts. He undressed and got into bed. If he had had a book he would have lighted a candle and tried to read, but he had no book, so he lay there, watching the moonlight on the casement and wondering what Miss Valentine's book could be all about, written by a Scottish gentleman in French, that she hid away from her father's eyes.

Robyn was now ready to spy offence in the smallest incident, and one of these happened the very next day. One of the master-carpenters had some knowledge of masons' work too, and once or twice lately Hendryk had consulted this man over some matter that formerly he would have discussed with Robyn. Such a matter arose, and Robyn, judging this a time to assert himself, put his spoke in. But Hendryk merely heard what he had to say, nodded, and went on talking to the carpenter as if he had not spoken. To make matters worse, it was not even certain that there would again be any meeting that evening, for her father might require her, and if she did not appear it would be like beginning everything all over again. That day he could not even settle down to his toad and burdock. He felt as he had felt on that first night of all, when he had waited down by the ha-ha, and away over the wide lawn that small pale figure had appeared like a moth in the dusk, and he had been left in an agony of guessing whether it was a signal or not.

And he still had to sit at the same table with Hendryk, but that very evening he cut the meal short. Rising without a word he walked round the chapel and out to the lawn, made a wide detour by the ha-ha, and reached the hedge. She was not there, but the light was burning behind the diamond panes, and to-night the light had a wakeful, dangerous sort of look. If it had gone suddenly out his heart would have given a leap, for how was he to know what watching eyes might have taken its place behind the glass, warned by some slight sound of what was afoot outside? And the sunken garden was even worse. Trapped there there would be no escape, and she was late, or perhaps unable to come, and he suddenly knew at what a peril he himself was there at all.

But as suddenly he again found himself growing desperate and bold. Hendryk had turned against him; on a point of stonework he set a carpenter's opinion before his own; but where was all that courage that should have been in his blood? Oh to have known just a little more of his father's story and the odds *he* must have struggled against and overcome! Own brother to homely John Skyrme, the younger of the two, yet acknowledged and bowed down before as the brethren in Genesis had humbled themselves in the presence of Joseph! Who had made the way easy for gallant Ned Skyrme, taking him by the hand and leading him to the highest seats? He had forced open his own doors, plucked his own flower, not from the nearest field or hedgerow, but from the closed and guarded garden itself, and was Robyn Skyrme going to shame such a father by turning craven now? Suddenly he heard a light footstep. It was three tiptoe paces only as she crossed the hard path and gained the safe softness of the grass, and there she stood at the top of the three steps, in trepidation to get down to the garden below.

But suddenly he stood in the way, turning her back and

shaking his head. No, not the garden, and she gave a quick glance over her shoulder at the lighted window.

'Then where?'

Without a word he drew her round the corner of the hedge past its furthest border, where she suddenly stopped, pulling aside the hawk-moth cloak she had passed over her head.

'Where are we going?'

'Anywhere – but not the garden —'

'It must only be a little way —'

'This way,' and a moment later the light from the house was no longer to be seen.

Behind the garden was a paddock, but this they skirted, for there the home farm began, and the high plantation, that was steep at its eastern end, fell away to a field of corn that was cut and stooked but not yet carried. Here the tangle of the wood thinned out to firs, behind which the moon would presently rise, and their flattened tops made dim mats against the sky, as if the cast-up seaweed of a beach had lodged and suspended itself there. Noiselessly he opened a gate, for a furlong away other lights now showed, the lights of the cottages where the hinds and labourers lived, but a moment later the high straggle of the hedge hid them again. Only then did she uncover her hooded face.

'Why wouldn't you go into the garden?'

'I don't know – I didn't want to —'

'But if they want me they'd never think of looking for me here —'

'I know,' and they walked forward again.

The lateness of the moon only sprinkled the heavens the more palely with their thin dust of stars. Soon they too would go, all but the greater ones, but over the fir-tops they still made a milky wake, and the cornfield beneath them had its own illumination. The stooks were shadowless, the gleaned stubble brittle with small sparkles. Now that she had uncovered her head its coronal of ribbons and curls seemed to have alighted on it from his own jack-o'-lantern, and where the firs came down to the cut corn he kicked over a stook with his foot. Without speaking they settled themselves against it.

But if he was blindly bold she was now as timorous. It must not be for more than five minutes, she said, but in that starry shadowless field the cloak made a dark patch against the pallor of the corn, and he sought to make it less visible.

'Was it only one night?' he asked when he had finished.

'What?'

'That I haven't seen you.'

'What did you do?'

'Pretended to work.'

'I told father to-night I should be back in a few minutes.'

'It doesn't matter what time I go in now.'

'Why?'

'I've been put in another room,' and she drew in her breath.

'Do you mean you asked Mistress Eleanor?'

'No. It was Hendryk. We've had a quarrel,' and she was silent for so long that he wondered whether she had heard.

'What did you quarrel about?' she asked at last.

'What do you suppose?'

'How should I know?'

'It was about you.'

'About me!'

'He doesn't say so, but it is that. He knows I love you.'

'I think I must go now.'

'Didn't you hear what I said?'

'Oh, I oughtn't to have come here.'

'Is that all?'

It was not all, for she let him take her hand, but her thoughts were elsewhere and even the two hands seemed to be sulking together.

'I liked the garden better than here,' she pouted.

'Why? Because you're afraid?'

'What is there to be afraid of?'

'I told you I loved you.'

'If he calls and I don't hear —'

'Is that all you care about?' and she snapped off an ear and began to nibble it.

But was it after no better fashion than this that his father had wooed, bickering and retorting, while the minutes slipped by, and behind the plantation the moon got up, and the pale stars overhead thinned out till only a few of the greater courtiers remained, and it really would be time she went back to the house? Had his mother pirtled and pouted about where she was told she was loved, in a dark and dangerous garden, or here among the stooks, where none would think of looking for them, and they could talk quite loud if they liked instead of breathing in whispers? Fie on you, Robyn Skyrme, to be as cross as two sticks when you ought to be putting your best foot foremost, and your softest and sweetest words at the top, as you would have done if it had been Miss Valentine, for be sure she would not have broken her heart about it, and to-morrow you too would have forgotten, and whistled at your work once more! Even if you cannot pretend to yourself that her image has never left you since that first Sunday morning at Mixton church-porch, you can tell *her* so, for it is that that they wish to hear, and even your father knew of no better way! So he turned to the sulking little head that nibbled the corn. He drew it nearer to his own and took the stalk from her fingers. Was it a heinous offence that ribbons tied into hair in the morning should be a little tumbled in a cornfield at night? Ribbons and ringlets, his hands were about them both, as they had never been in that box-hedged garden, and she began to murmur something, but did not finish.

Never let them finish those things, Robyn! Her father is

a studious man and will never notice. Even Mistress Eleanor need not see her hair if she slips into her chamber by some other way.

The first harm of lips was done before either of them spoke again.

'Sweetheart!' he breathed, taking away the hand that had already gone of itself to the disarranged head.

'Why did you do that?'

'Why did you make me?'

'I never —'

'You did – I hate that garden —'

'I hate it here —'

'Betty – call me Robyn —'

'I won't —'

'You *won't?*' And at the way he said it she could not help but laugh tremulously too.

Presently there was an alteration of the sky and a change on the cornfield's face. The fir-tops became a black wrack among their rusty boles; where the plantation ended a silver gleam shot across the farther stooks, and the stubble was in shadow, And soon he would be drawing that cockchafer cloak about her again instead of trying to make her shape the same colour as the corn, for when the moonlight crept round they too would be in shadow, and any hind returning late to his cottage might see the paler underwings beneath. But now, with the trusses whispering in their ears, they were little more than voices.

' – all those years ago —' he was murmuring in her ear.

'Father was at Mixton on one of his Commissions —'

'You had those green gloves on and a psalter in your muff —'

'How you remember!'

'And when I saw the chairman in the church at first I thought he was a robber, and I went three or four times after that, but nobody knew who you were —'

'You mean you asked people, as you asked Mistress Eleanor about me and Celia —'

'Celia! . . . Call me Robyn again —'

'R for Robyn —'

'Betty —'

It came, the moon's first enormous stare, turning the stooks to silvery white and black shadow, glistening on the stubble, washing the land with its inundation. It woke the birds in their nests, and there floated noiselessly past the owl that Robyn ought to have been carving for his capital. There was pain in the stubble too, for the nocturnal hunt was up, with small squeakings and cries, but no more talk was heard from where they lay. Though it had been in whispers, there had been far more of it in their arbour within a stone's throw of the house, and it may be that both of them knew that they would set foot in that sunken garden together no more. The moon had been new on that first night when he had spied her from down by the ha-ha. To-night it was full, and to-morrow night it would be on the wane.

20

AT midday the next day the workmen were sitting on the blocks about the outside pulpit, eating their midday meal. Robyn, inside the chapel, was still at work when he was aware of Hendryk, standing behind him. He now spoke to Hendryk only if Hendryk spoke to him, and as Hendryk did not speak he went on with his chipping.

But Hendryk looked as if he had not slept for a week, and things could not go on like that, and again Robyn was willing to say something conciliatory. He gave his capital a half-turn on its pivot, wedged the pivot again, and then said something about his design beginning to take shape at last. But his mallet was arrested in mid-air at the tone of Hendryk's reply.

'I've seen things taking shape this long time.'

'I meant my capital.'

'It was you I meant, not your capital,' and a glance at his face told Robyn all.

'He'll have finished his dinner by three o'clock,' Hendryk went on in the same expressionless voice. 'You're to go to his room at half-past. Mistress Eleanor will show you the way,' and Hendryk shambled out of the chapel again.

Robyn had no questions to ask. He stood for some moments looking at his toad and burdock-leaves, still unfinished, never by him to be finished. Then he picked up his chisels, slipped them into the pocket of his smock, cast a piece of sacking over the capital, rolled down his sleeves, and walked up to his own room.

He was not aware of any particular emotion. Had he been summoned to Colonel Firminger's room three months ago, in June, there might have been seals or sea-horses to discuss, or that drawing of the roof-ridge as it had been fifty years ago, or perhaps a word or two of commendation on the good report Hendryk had made of him. But now it was September, and the moon was past its full, and the roof ridge was not even begun. He wanted no dinner, and looked round the room. There on the wall hung his pack. It was empty, and removing his working-smock he disposed it about the tools he had bought in York in such a way that they should not clank and packed them into the bottom of it. Then he washed himself, scrubbing his hands till they were red, and got out his best clothes. At least he would depart in his best, changing perhaps into his older clothes again when he had left Maske behind him.

There was nothing to be read in Mistress Eleanor's face when, at half-past two, he presented himself before her. She might or might not have known his errand, and he had to sit in her room till she too made herself ready. Then, with her keys jangling at her waist, she led the way upstairs to the gallery, past the library, down the two steps of the floor and up again, and so to the farther angle beyond which he now saw for the first time. Here the passage turned along the western end of the house, and at an oaken door at the end of it Mistress Eleanor stopped. Beyond this door was another, at which she knocked and waited. A voice must have answered, for she pushed and stood back for Robyn to enter. Then she closed the door again behind him.

Colonel Firminger was sitting at his working-table with his back to the motionless Robyn. The latticed window on his left hand showed many papers spread out on the table, books of accounts, his quills and penknife, his inkhorn and sandbox, a number of apples, a whiplash, and other odds and ends, such as Sim Dacres was always mending in his far-away cottage at Unthank. But Robyn's eyes had gone instantly to the window. Over its low sill he could see the corner of the box-hedge below, and it was along the hedge that his eyes were travelling. But such observations were of little use to him now, and as his entry did not seem to have been heard he took a couple of steps towards the end of the table, standing respectfully back from it. Only then did the Colonel raise his head.

But to Robyn's surprise his face betrayed neither anger nor overwhelming grief. Indeed, he looked at Robyn as if something luckless rather than heavily blameworthy had alighted on him, the consequences of which he nevertheless could not escape. Careworn and responsible he looked, as if he saw in Robyn a well set-up and deserving lad, decently dressed, over whose chin a razor had yet to pass for the first time, who, whatever he chose to say, would have no word of reply. But his pen remained in his hand, at his elbow stood a leather bag of money, and whatever was to be done was evidently to be done with despatch.

'No doubt,' he began, 'Mistress Eleanor has told you why I have sent for you.'

'No, sir,' said Robyn.

'She has not?'

'I was only told to be here at half-past three, sir,' and this seemed to put the Colonel out of his stride, as if he must now find another beginning.

'Ah. Hm. But at least it comes as no surprise to you?'

'No, sir.'

'You have been well treated in this house?'

'Yes, sir.'

'There was nothing – up to this last fortnight – that you can advance as a reason – in short, as a reason for your being here now?'

Neither yes nor no came from Robyn now, and Colonel Firminger's tired eyes were meditatively on the window.

'If,' he said slowly, 'I had not had a full and true confession of this unseemly affair my attitude would naturally have been a different one. You are perhaps less to blame than others, and you are not the only one to suffer. The young woman also will not enter this house again.'

Robyn could hardly believe his ears. The young woman! Could Colonel Firminger be speaking in this cool and judicial way of his own daughter? But he went on.

'Before I even saw you – I refer to the first occasion when Mr Maas waited upon me – you were recommended to me as a young man of promising parts. Later I was able to judge of this for myself, and you will therefore be paid your just wages up to noon to-day. After that I have no further need of you. It is Miss Valentine I find it hardest to forgive, and I have written a letter to her father. I will not have my daughter made a go-between in such matters. As for yourself – I tell you this for your own good, for to possess certain gifts does not remove you from your proper station in life – do not, if you wish to be happy, feed your fancy on presumptuous dreams. It is not on your betters that the ruin will fall, but on yourself. I have spared her father as many of the details as I could, but – you were down in that garden last night?' and again his eyes rested on the window.

Dumbfounded, Robyn found not a word to say.

'As also you were – no, not the night before that, for my daughter was here with me – but before that, and again before that, and for the past fortnight and more?'

Still not a word rose to Robyn's lips.

'At least you do not lie, and I have had the whole story from my daughter this morning, that forward girl's message, your own youthful folly, and her own small part in it. I can only thank God it was no worse, and it only remains to pay you. Let me see. You and Mr Maas arrived here — ' and he sought among his papers to establish the date.

And even yet the full illumination might not have broken upon Robyn had not Colonel Firminger's disturbance of the papers uncovered what lay beneath them. His hand did not go to the whiplash; instead, a book lay looking up at Robyn from the desk. It was the book she had stolen into the library to fetch that torrid afternoon, taking it from behind the folio and walking out again with her buttercup head bent over it. It was the book she had from Miss Valentine, the book about the scandals of the Court, written by the Scottish gentleman in French, and now forced from her possession by her father.

That very morning she too had stood where he stood now, and because she was a gentlewoman and his daughter, but Robyn was a wage-man, the worst of the storm had broken over *her* head.

There she had stood, gulping and in tears, confessing just as much as she thought fit, and he had accepted her imposture about Miss Valentine, and thanked God it was no worse, and here the Steward now was, counting out ten pounds from the leather bag, and setting the pieces in a row and telling them off with his finger again, for he was a nearsighted man, and giving Robyn dispositions for his journey.

'I have given orders,' he said, 'and you will be accompanied as far as Scarswold and your horse brought back here. At Scarswold you will go to the Maske Arms, where you will find a second horse, that will post you as far as Low Kirby. After that your journey will be at your own charges. You will start at half-past four. Have you much to carry?'

Robyn, his head still spinning, could hardly get out his shaky 'No, sir.'

'A word more, for I have no wish to be harsh and you have your way to make in the world. If you are returning to York, Low Kirby will be somewhat out of your direction, so to that extent you may vary your journey. I understand that formerly you were a farmer. Is stonecutting now to be your trade?'

'Yes, sir,' Robyn choked, for other thoughts were surging in him now.

'In that case it would be hard if you were forbidden to speak of your work here. You may therefore tell your employers that for three months you worked at Maske. Where will go you if you fail to find employment at York?'

'Lincoln,' Robyn heard some other Robyn say.

'Mr Maas sees no reason why he should not remain here and finish his work. The old roof-ridge is not past restoration, and simpler capitals will serve. I hope your next venture will be a happier one, and that is all, except that I wish you no ill.'

But suddenly Robyn broke down as no girl would ever have broken down. From the window he had seen the box-hedge below, and the gap where the three steps descended to the garden, and into that garden the moon had looked, rising a little later each night, till it had peeped even into the dark little arbour at the end. It was in that garden that he was supposed to have been the evening before, and he wanted to drop on his knees at the table end, but his hand went to his neckcloth instead, for it seemed to be strangling him, and he did not know his voice for his own.

'Sir, oh sir! For just five minutes – for a minute – can't I see her before I go?'

But now that the Colonel had finished he gave him a quick, authoritative look. Was it all to be said twice?

'Who? My daughter? The letter I have written to Miss Valentine's father will explain all that is needed.'

'For a minute, sir – only for a minute — '

'Why?' the Colonel snapped, suddenly erect in his chair.

'Only – only — '

But the dangerous moment passed. Once more Colonel Firminger's eyes fell on the merry Scottish gentleman's book, that Robyn could not have read even if he had wished, because it was in French.

'No,' he said, and took up his pen again.

The door closed behind Robyn.

At twenty minutes past four that afternoon Hendryk Maas stood under his half-octagon of an outside pulpit, considering the bay of new tracery he had put in. The framework of the chapel roof looked like tip-to-toe fingers meeting at its ridge, and a yard or two away from Hendryk a mason was drilling a dowel-hole in the old broken dolphin. Hendryk saw Robyn's shadow on the grass, and turned, but seeing who it was did not speak.

'Good-bye, Hendryk,' said Robyn, and Hendryk put on his glasses.

'Are you off?'

'In ten minutes.'

'Back to York?'

'No. I think Lincoln way.'

'Then if you're Lincoln-bound you'll be passing through Mocklington. That window we did ought to be starting to weather soon.'

'It was our first job together,' said Robyn in a shaking voice.

'Mocklington? Ay, so it was,' said Hendryk.

'Shall you be here all the winter, and next summer?'

'Well, it's as good a place as another, and it's work,' and Robyn's eyes were moist.

'*Never* anything but work, Hendryk?'

'Well, work's a good stand-by,' said Hendryk thoughtfully. 'I remember you asked me once what my religion was, and I said sometimes it was Early Perpendicular and whiles a bit Flamboyant. But it's always work.'

'Good-bye, Hendryk.'

'That's it. Follow the horses. I hear 'em.'

'Aren't you going to shake hands?'

'Why not?' said Hendryk, and wiped his dusty hands on his apron, and shook hands with Robyn, and let the hand go again. Then, murmuring to himself 'Early Perpendicular, Early Perpendicular, but it's always work,' he rubbed his great nose and cocked his eyes up at his pulpit again. When next he looked round Robyn had gone.

21

NOT a flutter of a handkerchief, not a hand-wave from a window, but only Robyn on a horse, with a serving-man riding on either side of him, his back to Maske, and a tale borne back to the house if he as much looked round! Yet he did look round, for at least there were the tall clusters of twisted chimneys to take his farewell of, and the plantation behind that showed the inside of the courtyard, and its dropping away to the cornfield, where to-day they were carrying the stooks. His good-bye to Maske was no more than that, and as the road dipped suddenly to Easby village and the trees shut it out his thoughts came sluggishly to life again.

Suppose in her fear she *had* lied to her father? Could he reproach her for that? Nay, when he had brokenly asked whether he might not see her again, and Colonel Firminger had looked sharply up and rapped out a 'Why?', had not his own lie been as ready as hers? There were a thousand reasons why it had had to be a lie, when even a whisper of the truth would have been madness and ruin and a father's broken heart. It was infinitely better as it was; and yet – if only it *could* have been the truth! He flushed again with the indignity and the humiliation of it. A young miss's peccadillo, fluttering out from between the pages of some trivial gay book of the Court, a scolding that she would have forgotten in a week and himself packed off with his wages in his pocket so that all should be as it had been before – was it all to shrivel away to that? A valorous adventure, to be riding away between two mutes of serving-men, when Starlight ought to have been clattering the road carrying the pair of them! With her behind him he could then have risen in his good Ripon stirrups, and given a shout that would have brought the crows from their nests, and sent the rabbits bolting for their burrows, and white-faced lies back to the timid hearts that had hatched them! The danger, the pursuit, the shot, the tightening of her arms as he drove in the spurs, and if they were to die then let them die together – oh, where was she now and what were her thoughts? Locked in her chamber, sobbing into her pillow instead of whispering to him in the corn, and orders given that none should go near her, and a book sent back to the other's father with a letter, as if Robyn Skyrme's love had been an abject thing, as indeed it was now that it was brought so low! But as they rode through Easby village one of his conductors spoke across him to the other.

'Think you we shall make Scarswold this side of sunset, Thomas?'

'I misdoubt it,' the other replied.

'There'll be no moon till eleven.'

'And not a deal by then by the look o' yon wrack.'

'Colonel or no Colonel, I'm not starting back in the dark to-night, not with an extra horse to hold in,' the first growled, and his tone put it all on Robyn that they must be out and abroad when other people were in their beds, and on they trotted.

It was eight o'clock before the lights of Scarswold pricked the twilight, and the lights seemed to hearten his attendants, for here one of them addressed Robyn for the first time, in a not unkindly, or it might have been an inquisitive voice.

'It isn't every stonemason that's set off in such style as this, young man. What have you been up to?' But that was a question Robyn was not answering.

'Ask him when you get back,' he said shortly, and the man gave a haw.

'Him? The Colonel? And be given the key of the road myself?'

'No. Mr Maas,' said Robyn, for his thoughts had turned to Hendryk now, and those few sparse words of farewell was his cruellest humiliation of all. But if Hendryk answered any questions it would be to put down Robyn's dismissal to his own idleness and shiftlessness, and the more he thought of it the more he found to be said for such answers, no matter whose the lips that spoke.

'Well, you know what you're to do when we leave you?'

'What?' said Robyn.

'Scarswold's as far as the Maske writ runs. If the moon clears we shall start back to-night, but maybe we shalln't, and the posting's in ten-mile stages. Where are you bound for?'

'Mocklington and across the Humber, then Lincoln.'

'Peter Lumby of the Maske Arms will tell you the best roads. All the horses are branded, but that isn't to say an odd one doesn't go astray now and then, and I should stick to the daytime if I was you. Do you carry anything?'

'If you mean a pistol, yes.'

'Then put something over that jacket and neckcloth. There's sharp eyes on the roads. Make out you're like us, taking a horse back or something. Have you broke your indentures?'

Some keystone in Robyn seemed to slip and settle again, not in its former place. When two sportive young gentlewomen peeped into a forbidden book, and mischief followed, there was no stripe for stripe or burning for burning for them. A little dust in a father's eyes, a young man sent about his business, and Hendryk would bear him out in his falsehood.

'Yes,' he said. 'I broke my indentures. Tell them all that,' and they drew up under the blazoned signboard of the Maske Arms.

That he was a ne'er-do-well prentice, who had broken his bond with his master and was lucky to get away as lightly as he did, was evidently the account they gave of him to Peter Lumby of the Maske Arms, for Robyn, seated in a dimly-lighted corner with his pack between his knees, saw the three of them glancing at him over the hatch as they discussed him and his misdoings. But the Maske corn was to carry, and the sky had cleared and the moon shone boldly out, and the two men had decided to get back that night after all. They nodded a good night to Robyn as they passed through the bar to where the horses stood at the door, and the friendlier of the two wished him a prosperous journey. But just as he was setting foot in the stirrup he withdrew it again and returned.

'I'd wellnigh forgotten,' he said. 'He said I was to give you this,' and into Robyn's hand he thrust Hendryk's parting gift, a case-flask of something, schiedam belike, to set him on his way.

Just a flask of numbing strong water to take the place of all, all, all – the gift was almost more than Robyn could bear. He himself could hardly believe that up to that very moment he had been hoping for something else, from somebody else, a note perhaps slipped into his hand or a yellow ribbon from her hair.

But it was only a flask of liquor, and once more he sat in the half-lighted bar, gazing at the pack between his knees.

The next morning he had other things to think of. Scarswold neighboured on the abbey-lands, but Robyn never wanted to see the abbey-lands again, and as Peter Lamby was a Maske tenant it was safe to consult him not only about the way he must take, but also about the changing and disposal of the money Colonel Firminger had counted out to him. And here again he had fallen among well-disposed people. The horse that Peter Lumby provided would take him as far as Low Kirby, but he had been warned after that his travelling must be provided out of his own pocket, and after Low Kirby he would have to change from horse to horse every ten miles, unless by some chance it fell out otherwise. All this Peter told him, mapping him out a way, and Mistress Lumby, who whenever she looked north from her own door saw the road winding away in a known direction, but south into the hostile and unknown, spent half that morning in unpicking and restitching his clothes to give him the appearance of a wayfaring man. She was a large and comfortable-hearted woman, and she fussed over him as she patted his person, all over which his changed money was distributed in little packets.

'There!' she said as she stood back to look at him, dressed in an old waggoner's hat, his mason's smock all changed about, and furnished with a great staff for a weapon. 'Put a wisp of straw in your hat and anybody's think you were off to a hiring! But keep a good heart, that's the main, and always remember when one door closes another opens!'

So Robyn left the Maske writ behind him, and the last he saw of it was the great blazon of the Maske Arms, swinging over the inn door.

The Low Kirby stage was a short one, but he decided to go no further that afternoon. He was now a journeyman-mason in search of employment, Colonel Firminger had graciously given him leave to say that for three months he had worked at Lord Maske's private chapel, and if he wished to change his direction for York here was the place where he must do so. But York was now the last place he wanted to see. In York he would be thinking of Miss Valentine, and to think of Miss Valentine would be to think of the other, and anywhere or anything now, but not that. He must be thinking of the little things, and even before he had left Low Kirby he was able to see how differently different travellers were received, and how those of substance came first and those on foot with packs on their backs must take what was left. Horses were plentiful enough, but such as he were sent from inn to inn before they could bargain even for an animal of so known a character that it bore not one branding, but three or four, so often had it changed hands. He must learn too to keep his hands from going to his concealed pockets in that betraying way, for it seemed to him that too many strangers were forward to talk to him, and even less to his liking, he had to talk to them, and he remembered Hendryk's talk of catchpoles and runaway prentices, and how the inns were full of those who would have sold him for a shilling. It had been an easy thing to sit waiting for Hendryk on an alehouse bench, watching the lads at play on some green, and to see his mixture-flushed face as he had come shambling up, rubbing his hands and saying 'We start to-morrow, Robyn!' The nearest place where his own name would now have any credit would be Mocklington, and that name was now Waygood, and now that he found himself face to face with it, even a great church like Mocklington would not need a new north window every few years.

So a certain Robyn Waygood began to look for work as a mason on his own account and to wonder by what magic Hendryk had done it. No doubt it was a feather in the cap of one so young that he was able to say that he had worked at York, but even this was not Germany and the Netherlands and Brabant, and when he presented himself before master-masons (for higher than these he dared not yet approach) he had countless questions to answer about himself, where he came from, why he had left, what masons he knew in the neighbourhood, what was his guild-branch. And when the master-mason shook their heads, but passed him on to their betters to be rid of him, at first his heart was filled with hope, for at the mention of Hendryk's name up went the brows of deans and prebends, and smiles alighted on their lips, and they too began to ask him questions. Hendryk Maas! He had learned his trade from Hendryk Maas! A notable character! Hardly in a generation, they agreed, was such a man to be met with, such a craftsman, such an artist at heart, but ah – and then would come a sigh. And he was building a new chapel at Maske? The tragedy it was that he was so unaccommodating, so prickly to handle! If only he had been able to defer a little more to the opinions of others, their mistaken opinions perhaps, instead of being always so right himself and everybody else so wrong! It was not good for the general advancement that he should have all that rightness to himself. The Guilds had extended the hand of fellowship to him, but he had seen fit to scorn it, and as for Robyn himself – to be brought under such a dangerous influence at the very beginning of his career – and another headshake would be the end of the matter.

So Robyn began to use the name of Hendryk Maas less and less. He put that of Mechlin Tom in its place, and again Mocklington became the only place ungleaned by the all-devouring Guilds. But at Mocklington his name had been neither Waygood nor Skyrme, and try as he would he could not remember what name he had taken when he had helped Hendryk with the north window, but nevertheless it was towards Mocklington that his face was turned.

He was making for the flat lands and the coast, for it seemed a lifetime since he had smelt the cold sharp smell of the sea or seen the flicker of the sheldrake or heard the harsh cry of a gull. He had forgotten the guillemots and their clumsy eggs, the thin-shanked oyster-catchers, the flighting duck at eve and the cloud-sheen in the wide wet sands. Yet as he drew further and further south none of these things seemed the same, for the land in which he now found himself was a land without a shore. No sea-wall had been set up against the inundations here, no marge of shingle or sand divided the ground under his feet from the ocean beyond. All he came upon was an edge and a drop. Approach that edge in fog or fret and your next step would be upon nothing, not even the wrinkled high-water mark of weed or wrack, but only the abrupt talus fallen into the tide. Two yards each year they said the sea took, with whatever was on it, crop or churchyard, seamark or common or cottage, so that the population had left, and only empty houses awaited their end, and the only church bells here were those the fishermen said they sometimes heard on still nights, rising from the sunken shoals that had once been the habitations of men.

So as there was no work for Robyn here he turned about again, but inland he fared little better. Either he must dip into those small packets Mistress Lumby had stitched into his clothes or take the scanty work that offered to a foot-plodder like himself, a field of muck to spread or a tree to fell, a stopped drain to clean out or a miry road to fill in. A bed and a collop were most of his wages, and always there were the questions about himself, who he was and where he came from and what he was doing there.

But what the sea took it cast up again, and he did not leave that desolate region till he had seen distant Spurn, whittled away to seaward but all paid back again by the restless tides, that deposited it again at Sunk Island, where a wilderness of stakes marked the creeks and channels, and across the mud of the banks and the white of the breakers and the tossing of multitudes of birds Lincolnshire's low line could be faintly seen.

And it was the older, the farther back things that began again to stir in Robyn's sluggish blood now, not the spell of the past few months or years. Sometimes, mounted on whatever screw or cast-off he had been able to hire, he would draw in the animal, and sit in the saddle gazing north, trying to tell himself that only so many posts away was York, with its busy stoneyard, and Mechlin Tom and the rest of them still at their stone-scouring and pointing and chipping, and the melancholy spectacle of the weed-grown abbey-lands. Over there was Maske, and Hendryk and his outside pulpit, and in its barns the heavy flails would be thudding now, and soon they would be ploughing in the stubble again, the stubble that had glistened so under the full moon. But just as he was flinching from the memory of insupportable things they would fade away in some curious way of themselves, and other images would come instead, of that flat line beyond the birds and the stakes that was Lincolnshire, and of Umpleby Stattis to which he had once skated in a day, and what they were all doing at Unthank now. If he was going to Lincoln he would have to pass that way, and far more sharply and clearly than Maske's roofs and twisted chimneys he could see its steadings again, and the yard where they had burnt the ricks, and the house itself, its white upper parts floating of an evening like a boat on its under-walling of flints. So Unthank's common hall and his own chamber under the belfry he might presently see again, but a close-clipped box-hedge, with a break in it and three stone steps that led down to a sunken garden – never.

But the boy Robyn Skyrme was the man Robyn Waygood now, settled in stature and the knowledge his wanderjahre had brought him. In those days he had run away from fear, but anybody looking at him now, with that fair sprouting on his chin and look of set watchfulness and readiness in his blue eyes, the staff Peter Lumby had given him and a hidden pistol to boot, might very wisely beware of him. One other thing too he had learned from inns and other places where all-comers talk together. This was that the men could be outfaced, but that the women, of whom there was no lack, were best avoided altogether. It was no business of theirs who he was nor where he came from nor what he had left behind him. He was on his way to Mocklington, where the prebend knew him, and would (he hoped) give him letters to Lincoln.

22

HE did not know the name of the village at which he fetched up at four o'clock of an October afternoon, on foot, for a carter had given him a useful lift that morning and he had no wish to make too long a day of it. If there was a horse to be had he hoped to be in Mocklington the next day, and at

Mocklington, Hendryk had told him, the north window ought to be weathering by now. He would have to use Hendryk's name to the prebend; he had been thinking of this all the afternoon as he had walked; but he felt that he owed Hendryk a longer and more difficult explanation than the weathering of his north window. His wanderings had taught him that to ask at most inns for ink and paper was to be met with a stare, so he carried his own small supply with him. But first make sure of his supper and a bed, for he had not eaten since breakfast, and arriving on foot his bed might well be bracken-litter or a truss of straw.

So at this village of which he did not know the name he made his customary play with a separate portion of his money, that it might not be thought he was a penniless person, frowned, stroked his downy chin, and asked what was for supper. The man he addressed, evidently the landlord of the place, had a large and sickly and foolish-looking face, and though his inn seemed dilapidated and poor it did not surprise Robyn that in such a country he had the choice of various wildfowl, and he ordered that a teal should be put on the spit. Then, since it had become a habit with him never to make himself too comfortable till he had first had a good look at his whereabouts, he walked out into the street again till his supper should be ready.

The first thing he noticed as he looked up was that the inn out of which he had just stepped bore no sign. There projecting above his head was its iron bracket, with the rusty hooks still in it, but the board had gone, for it stood in an exposed place and as likely as not some gale had carried it away. And the next thing he noticed was the fewness of lights and people and the wretched impoverishment of the farming, for all about was bad land, a plague of thistles had advanced upon the whole village, and it could be but scratching for a living at the best. Indeed, a number of roofs had fallen in completely, windows were empty or boarded up, and from what had been plots and gardens the thistles had spilled over into the street itself in a way that John Skyrme would have wept to see. But at the foot of the street was a market-cross and a second inn, and this bore a sign-board, at which Robyn stepped back to look. Its nearer side was scoured to an illegible grey-white, which again seemed to show the direction from which the sea-winds came, but its other side was fresher, and showed a woolpack tied at its corners. But every window was closely shuttered, and when Robyn tried the hasp he found the Woolpack's door locked. Then a man who was talking to another man called to him from across the street.

'It's no good your trying there, maister. It's been shut this five year.'

'What's the name of this village?' Robyn called back.

But the man only went on talking to his companion, and it was not Robyn's business to tell him that his supper was already cooking elsewhere, and he passed on to the small square and its cross.

And here he had expected to find the church, but there was no church, and still he did not see more than three or four people. But this was hardly to be wondered at, for it was drawing on for six o'clock, the sky was heavily overcast, sensible people were at their firesides, and from several chimneys he saw a thin rising of smoke. Again he asked the name of the village, this time of a mangy-looking barefoot lad, and was told it was called Intake.

'Where's the church?' he asked, for it was his trade to known where churches were, and the lad pointed vaguely.

'Over there. It's four miles,' he said.

'How far is it from here to Mocklington?'

But either the lad did not know or he went to ask somebody, for he disappeared into a doorway, and did not return, and Robyn made his way back to his inn, having seen all of Intake there was to be seen.

He had swaggered into the inn with something of a bluster, in order that none arriving on a horse should be set before himself, but now the preparations that had been made in his short absence told him how few travellers of any kind at Intake must be made. An hour ago there had been no fire in the room; now dry wood cracked up the chimney, with a pile of branches for its replenishment. On a three-legged table between the hearth and the window were a platter and half a loaf, a knife and a pewter flagon. Fresh rushes had been thrown on the floor, and on these a great lurcher had made his bed, slinking in for the warmth of the fire, from which the vacant-faced landlord kicked him away. The room was the inn's public parlour too, for under the window and a long one wall were rough benches, and two barrels stood on a double gantry, and on a dresser were mugs and other vessels for service. But as the dry wood burnt away the green branches were slow in catching, and there was a shut-up feeling about the place, and gladly would Robyn have been in the kitchen where his teal was cooking, for where the pot and spit are there is the comfort too. But he judged it best to remain where he had been put, and for all he was tired he now never took his boots off till he had barred his chamber door and got into bed, so he put his pack under his stool and his staff in the corner, and as he waited to be served wondered what he should write to Hendryk after he had eaten.

The landlord himself brought in his teal, and as Robyn set about it with fingers and knife he again asked the questions to which he had had such scanty answers outside. But the man only opened a gap of a mouth and nodded. Evidently he was too witless to give him the information he sought. The teal was fat and sweet, though no sauce or side-dish went with it, but only the stale half loaf. So Robyn mused as he munched. 'Intake.' That meant that something had been hard-won or come by, as 'Unthank' meant disfavour; but this ungracious and slatternly village had not even kept what it had won. He would not have been eating teal if such fare had not provided itself from the neighbouring marshes, and the little he had seen told the same story. Four miles from its own church, the decent inn shut up and only this alehouse without a name left open, the broken and mouldering roofs, the thistles seeding themselves in the street and the grudging and unmannerly people – it could only mean that the industrious and thrifty had taken their husbandry elsewhere, leaving behind them only the bone-idle and the shiftless, those who waited for things to come to them, and if they didn't come slipped back in their nature themselves.

So ran Robyn's thoughts as first one and then another of them dropped in on him at his supper, called 'House!' for the landlord to come and serve them, and watched him as he ate. He would have preferred his own company, but none the less he finished his teal, the whole of it, sucking the juice from the bones and throwing them to the dog, and then stretching out his feet to the fire, which had taken a turn and was now crackling smokily. And even in this uncompanionate company it was better to talk, for not to talk is to draw attention to one's self, so he returned to his questions about the place, what were its history and its trade and what better days it had seen.

But they eked out their answers as they eked out their ale, and it did not occur to Robyn that, contrary to his experience of inns, while he asked them questions they asked him none. For some reason, he gathered, most of Intake's trade had been with the regions through which he had already passed, and once more the encroaching sea was at the bottom of it all. As it had continued to take its two yards each year the menace had preceded it like a shadow, and first this farmer had sunk beneath his burden of debt and had had to turn off his hinds, then the shops had begun to close their doors. None had mended his portion of the old road, and as the going got worse travellers had sought other ways round. There was no building a wall against the curse of thistles, and so Intake had been taken back again, and Robyn ceased his questions, and again sat looking into the fire, for he still had not made up his mind what he was going to say to Hendryk.

But he was brought out of his musing by an odd little incident. Again one of the inhabitants of the place had called 'House!' but this time it was not the landlord who entered. There appeared in the doorway instead as ill-fashioned a dwarf of a girl as Robyn had ever set eyes on. She was hardly more than four feet high, and her figure seemed the stumpier by reason of her having no neck. When Jessie Byers had knotted herself up in a head-cloth it had given her head a small and neat and gamesome look, but this girl's house-cloth was as pudding-like and lumpish as if her head grew directly out of her shoulders, and when she drew the ale Robyn saw that she did so with one hand only, setting the pot on the floor till it filled, for her other hand was in motion all the time, jigging up and down like sandhoppers when the tide ebbed and the great jelly-fish wasted away in the sun and what became of them after that only the next tide knew. But Robyn's own eyes were not bluer than those pale pools that looked forth from her misshapen head, and suddenly he thought of Polly Dacres and her ell-women who lived in holes in the river-bank, and felt slightly faint at what different shapes women could take and still be women.

And this afflicted creature had evidently taken over the serving from her father, for after that he did not appear again, and Robyn looked the other way whenever she entered.

Then, as the company had appeared one by one, so one by one they began to depart again. Soon only a couple of them remained, but even in the presence of these Robyn was not going to get out his pen and ink-horn, for they would have exchanged glances, as much as to say 'What have we here?' So he waited for them too to go, which presently they did, and by half-past eight Robyn was alone again, and he had now thought of his beginning to Hendryk, so he got paper from his pack, and set it on the three-legged table, and to his letter he set himself. Slowly he wrote:

> 'On a Thursday, from Intake, between the sea and Mocklington, which place I am in hopes of reaching to-morrow:
>
> 'Dear maister and friend: I have much to say to you, but this is not the time, and that you want to know about the window at M'ton will be put in when I get there. I have not found work yet, having seen no masons these past weeks, and missed Selby by reason of journeying along of a team of clothiers, the which place was out of their way. But of my savings I still have 3 lib. iiij d. and well in health. I prayed the men who saw me on my way from M. to carry a message which I hope they gave you —'

He had got as far as this when again he heard the opening of the door, and put his elbow over his letter. Once more it was the daughter of the inn – and yet was it? Except that there could hardly be two such dwarfs in Intake he would not have been sure, but it could only be she, and now what fantastic picture was this? Instead of the duster she had now clapped a top-heavy crimson turban on her head. It had a great jewelled gewgaw in front of it, like the mountebanks who had strutted and postured at Umpleby Stattis, and her bodice was of silver-embroidered green velvet, as was her kirtle, and the palsied hand flashed with the jewels of half a dozen rings. The outlandishness was made the more dreadful by the palpitations where her now uncovered neck should have been, like the gulping of a frog, and the ell-woman-blue eyes were on his writing as if it had been some diabolical and fascinating art. Had she changed herself so for *his* sake? Yet with it all she carried a kitchen brush, and crossed to the hearth and began to sweep it up.

There could be no more letter-writing in this distracting presence, and the rest of Hendryk's letter must wait till to-morrow. But for all his pity and loathing, Robyn remembered his civility, and asked her what time the inn closed its doors, and whether he was keeping her and her father out of their beds, and suddenly she giggled, her father's giggle, and the eyes under the turban stole round as she swept.

'Did you finish all that teal?' she asked, and Robyn nodded, supposing her to be wondering at his appetite.

'Yes. All of it,' he answered.

'I plucked it. *And* I cooked it. I've a clever hand at those things.'

'You have indeed,' Robyn humoured her, but wished none the less that any other hand had dressed the food he had put into his mouth, and her eyes rested on his ink-horn and paper again.

'Do you mean you can write?' she asked him with a kind of vacant awe. 'Letters to people, that they can have read to them?'

'Yes, if they can't read themselves.'

'Like the abram-men used to?'

'Yes.'

'For anybody? Could you for me?'

Robyn looked at her pitiful finery again, at the gewgaw in her turban and the jumping jewelled hand. What a merciful thing it was that these were spared the knowledge of their own state! Polly Dacres and her vanity of hair-brushing, this cripple whose only beauty was the wintry blue of her eyes! Then he smiled.

'Do you mean a letter to a sweetheart? Why, how old are you?'

At her reply – that she was forty – he had a little creeping of the skin. Forty! And he had taken her for fourteen! But this miserable inn had done its best for him, and he must make what return he could, so he told her that he would write any letter for her she wished.

'Now?' she cried eagerly. 'To my mother?'

'Yes, and I have wax, and you can make your own mark on the seal,' he answered as if in spite of her forty years she still had to be amused like a child.

Her eyes danced like a cold sun on ice. Dragging up a stool, she placed herself opposite Robyn. She had to clutch the table edge to keep the gaudily-ringed hand still, and she watched Robyn's every movement as he put his own letter aside, examined his pen and took a second sheet of paper. Then he sat waiting for her to begin.

23

BUT this she seemed far too excited to do. She had made up the fire with the green wood again, and some waft down the chimney brought the smoke back into the room. The lamp in its sconce seemed to be running out of oil, and she must have left the door only half fastened, for the lurcher entered, this time to sniff at Robyn's legs. Robyn thrust the creature away, but he next turned to his pack under the table, and when Robyn drove him away again retreated and showed his teeth. Robyn, who had fed the brute not an hour before, got up and opened the door, making a sound for the animal to get out, but the next moment he had forgotten the dog, for it seemed to him that he heard sounds from behind the closed door that faced him across the entrance-passage. It was there that his dinner had been cooked, but no light showed, and he had supposed the last of the company to have left half an hour ago. Yet from behind the door had come the low murmur of voices. Thrusting the dog out he closed the parlour door again and returned to his letter-writing.

But still the forty-year-old woman he had taken for a girl had not made up her mind what she wanted to say. She had got as far as 'My own mother,' but no further, and after he had twice encouraged her to go on he put down his pen, that she might take her own time. As he did so his attention was caught by sounds from the street outside. Some little way down it horses were starting off, and this reminded him of the horse he wanted to hire to take him to Mocklington on the morrow.

'How are you placed for horses here?' he asked her, but she only wagged her bedizened head.

'We don't keep horses at this inn.'

'But there must be horses in Intake.'

'Not a many,' she said.

'What's the name of this inn?'

'It used to be called the Sunrise.'

'Used to be? But it's an inn now. People come in and buy ale and sit down and drink it.'

'You must ask my brother,' she said.

'Is the landlord your brother?'

'Aye,' she answered.

'What's your name?'

'Moggy.'

'Moggy what?'

'Moggy,' and Robyn took up his pen again.

'Well, Mistress Moggy, if that's all the name you have, when people write letters they address them to somebody. Is your mother's name Moggy too?'

'No.'

'Then what am I to put outside it?'

'It will be took to her,' Moggy replied, and at that moment there was the unmistakable sound of a cautious step across the outer passage and the closing of a door. For a moment Robyn sat listening for further sounds. Then he pushed away his paper.

'What was that?' he asked.

'What?' she mumbled.

'Somebody's just gone out.'

'It was only Hobby, going to lock up.'

'Is Hobby your brother?'

'For sure he is.'

'And who were the men who were sitting here drinking?'

'They live here.'

'And where have they gone?'

'Home. There aren't a many places to go to in Intake.'

'Is that the kitchen across the passage, where you cooked the teal?'

'Aye,' was the answer, but the jewelled hand was jumping and knocking on the table edge now, so that she had to clap the other over it to keep it still.

'Then answer me a question. A quarter of an hour ago I heard two horses starting off for somewhere, and I've been watching those blue eyes of yours, looking up at that window, just behind me where I can't see without getting up. Those men, where have they gone?'

But at this the afflicted creature only broke into a heartrending wail – 'Oh, oh! And nobody's ever written a letter for me, and I want one sent to my mother, that's dying!'

So, Robyn Waygood or Skyrme, with your eyes already half opened, why are you wasting the precious minutes here, when you have only to drag that crimson clout from her head, and turn it into a gag for her mouth, and slip your pack on and be out of that door and in the thistle-seeded street and let any get within reach of your staff who can? You have learned that women are more dangerous than men, but is it only the young and yielding who hold a man's life and death in their eyes? Because one of them has split open your heart, are the treacherous and the pitiless to have what is left flung to them? You will find no mercy in those icy eyes that steal to the window because they know what is going on outside, and why those horses left, and why you heard sounds from the kitchen across the passage, and now linger over their letter because every minute gained is a minute shorn off your life! Swagger in your young manhood if you like, but do not forget those fears when you were a boy! There was nothing in them to be ashamed of, but shame on you if you take life on trust now that you know what it is! Remember you are in Holderness, where a long time ago you misheeded a warning, and told a secret to Starlight in her stall, and two of these died at the hands of your kindred, and such as they carry a stone in their pocket, and at the end of seven years turn it, but always fling it in the end!

So see to yourself while you can, for your comings and goings have never been hidden for long. Why, wherever you went, have you been questioned, but not questioned here? They might not have sought you out in York, for York is a great way off, but come into their own territory of yourself and none but God can help you.

Yet somehow there is a goodness in us that cannot believe in wickedness, because it is the wickedness that seems the phantasm and the hideous dream. Again she lifted those eyes that in the expiring firelight and the smoking of the spent lamp seemed to float in their own light, lent to her on earth like the rest, but for all eternity alive with bale.

'Oh, oh – and she's dying, and I want to send a letter to her!'

Robyn drew his paper towards him again. One by one the faltering words began to fall:

> 'My own mother, we are just going to bed and Hobby went snaring to-day and caught two teals. I have just cooked one for a young traveller who has come in from the north. It is him that is writing this letter for me. He is going to bed, too, and Hobby says your pains is cruel bad —'

But between her mother's pains and her struggle to compose her letter her mind seemed to lose itself again, and Robyn tried to help her out.

'What is your mother ill of?' he asked, and at the thought of her mother's sufferings she puffed suddenly out with pride.

'Ooooh! I hope *I* never have them like that! Cruel bad! I once saw her so bad with 'em she caught hold of her eye corner, here, and tore it open right down her cheek, like this!' And such was her mimicry of the ugly thing that he saw the veining of the back of her own eyeball in its pink socket. 'But ooooh, the grand clothes she has, rings and crowns and rubies and owches! — '

'Well – you'd got as far as her pains — '

But the pains were as far as that fatal letter ever did get, for the next instant Robyn had leapt to his feet and made a swift reach for his staff in the corner. Outside in the street he had again heard the hubbub of voices, horses, dismounting. The dwarf too had sprung up in a kind of ecstasy.

'It's my coach come for me!' she exclaimed with glee.

But already Robyn was out in the passage and flinging open the kitchen door.

Yet any whispering assembly that had been held that evening within its walls had long since broken up. As, long ago, Watty the fenman had gone his round by the Saltings and the Spit, meeting Robyn by the sea-wall and bidding him warn them at Unthank, so the men of Intake had dispersed to spread their flaming news. His way into the kitchen was barred by the snarling lurcher, but beyond he could see the pots and pans of the hearth, the remains of the landlord's supper on the table, and the moonstruck lout himself, hardly less gaudily-attired than his sister. He was standing over by the chimney, and clapped on his head was a coronet of gold. An ermine tippet was clasped about his shoulders, and round his waist he had tucked the satin shoulder-sash of an order, and he too had heard the sounds outside, for he raised his voice.

'Is that the coach, Moggy?'

'Aye, brother,' the dwarf's voice called back, and as Robyn moved the lurcher gave another ferocious growl.

But something untoward had happened about the coach, for somewhere behind Robyn an angry altercation was going on, in which Moggy's voice was shrilly raised. Turning, Robyn saw a slack-mouthed, cadaverous ruffian in a leather jerkin, cringing low before her as he sought to allay her fury.

'All the springs was broke, and half the spokes gone from one wheel, your royal highness; it hasn't been used for such a time —'

'Why were they broke? Who broke the springs of my royal coach?' and her voice now was that of a virago.

'He's being whipped now, Princess – he'll be whipped till you tell 'em to stop —'

'Why didn't you get another? Are there no coaches on the road?'

'There wasn't time, your highness —' and the screaming broke down into a blubber.

'Oh, and I wanted to go to Court in my coach! Hobby, do something to Jenkyn – I wanted my coach and he hasn't brought it!' But the man in the jerkin had backed away and was standing behind Robyn. Robyn felt his breath as he spoke close to his ear.

'Well, young maister, we'd about given you up,' he said, while Robyn, who had never seen his face before, wondered where before he had heard that voice. 'We're all of us a bit older than we were, but there's some things is none the worse for keeping. And what make *you* in Holderness?'

'Who are you?' said Robyn with a sinking heart, for he was on the point of remembering, and yet he was sure he had never seen this death's-head of a face; but the ell-woman stood between them, her eyes sparkling like the diamonds in her turban, which Robyn now saw to be real ones.

'You'll hear who *he* is when we get you to the Court, my bonnie lad!' she screamed. 'Maybe you'll wish you hadn't asked then! Perkyn they call him, and him that snared your teal, he's my brother, the Duke of Spurn, and *I'm* the princess Moggy, her majesty's oldest daughter!'

The men who had crowded into the passage closed in on Robyn.

24

FAR more diligently than he had said his prayers, it had been Robyn's first morning and evening care to draw the wad of his single pistol, empty the barrel of its charge, load it again and see to the priming of its pan. But it was not even a horse-pistol, that could be double-charged without bursting. It could only be fired once, and its chief virtue now was that none knew he carried it. His staff had been wrenched from his grasp, his wits alone could serve him, he knew that at the least show of resistance he would be bound, and the less he said, too, the better it would be for himself. They had brought horses, so he supposed they would mount him on one of them. With a horse under him there was still a chance, and it did not appear that he was to be blindfolded. Again Moggy was railing that no coach had been brought to fetch her. Her brother had taken off his coronet and cast a wrap over his finery, and was putting out the lights of the inn. Robyn was out in the street, and somebody was prodding him with his own staff in the back. A lantern was shone on the loop of a rope stirrup, and into this he was bidden to thrust his foot. Hobby turned the key in the door and was being helped into the saddle. Moggy was hoisted up behind him, and in silence they set forth.

Doors stood open as they descended the village street, and women thronged out of them to watch them pass. As they reached the shuttered inn and the market-cross a few lads fell in behind them and kept them company a little way, but in silence, and now that the still lamenting Moggy was denied her coach it had apparently been decided to take a short cut, for at the cross they left the village behind and to their right. A single barn, the broken roof of which reminded Robyn for a moment of the chapel at Maske, was the last of it to be seen, and now it appeared why he had been neither blindfolded nor bound. A month before the waste of heath that opened before them must have been flagrant with the beggarly purple of the thistles, as these miscreants bore their grotesque titles of Prince and Duke and Earl; but now, beneath the light of a low and sullen moon, all was as dun as a donkey's back, with only rags of fleece here and there to catch its waning light, and the fruits rotted on bramble and thorn, and the dim scamper of feeding rabbits at their approach. Through such a warren he needed both his eyes and his hands to guide his horse. They had been careful, too, to give him an animal that coughed and limped, and each of the men on either side of him carried a lantern and a loaded dag at half-cock, so that he could hardly have escaped even if he had been minded to make a bolt for it. They themselves presently seemed to think that the road might have been the better way after all, for after a time the horses dropped to a walk, and a man on foot went ahead, and the ground gave out a sucking noise, and the moon was hidden behind the crest as they had dipped to a shallow bottom.

Already with the checkings and windings Robyn had lost

his sense of direction. As there had been little rain all this marsh and water must come from elsewhere. Intake could not be so far from the sea but that creeks and branches made their way far inland, and he was splashing through shallow water skinned over with weeds and slime, where frogs drummed and rat-like life abounded, and the heads of the waterfowl were capped with green when they emerged from the surface. Gleams among lily-pads alternated with dim growths of reeds, and Moggy's voice ahead did not cease to threaten further punishment to the wretch who had neglected the care of her coach. But presently the land again rose a little, once more level with the moon, and Robyn's eyes were darting ahead, seeking for any vestige of a track or straight line that looked as if it had been planned by man. By flinging himself from his horse he might be able to take to the water and the reeds, where the horses could not follow.

But his hope died again. As they gained the crest he saw before him only an illimitable woolly lake of mists, spreading away and losing itself on three sides of him, that the track of the moon stained here and there in wisps of brown ironmould. But a mile away, keeping up from it, were the four ears of a dim church tower, capped by a short spire. Apparently it was for this that they were making, for ahead the Duke made a sound to his horse, and again Robyn's hopes rose. Where there was a church there was likely to be a road, and a score yards of fog between him and them would be even better than taking to the reeds. With a sound horse and his staff he might have chanced it even then, but he kept his head, and they began the descent into the mists.

Suddenly the light of the Duke's lantern died out. The men on either side of Robyn had closed in, but they too were no more than half-obliterated shapes, and somewhere to his right a horse missed its step and there was a growled curse and a splashing of water. 'Bear right!' a voice called, and suddenly Robyn's horse too stumbled. But his chance had gone without his knowing it. Close ahead a dull glare of rusty light showed, and the cavalcade stopped. There was a jostling as the horses fell into file. 'Duck your heads!' somebody shouted, and Robyn's own head fetched up violently against stone. Momentarily stunned, he closed his eyes.

He knew when he opened them again that they had arrived at their destination.

Countless as were the churches he had spent his life among during the past years, this was the first time he had ever ridden into a church on a horse, and as the muffling of the mists outside thinned suddenly away he put his hand to his bruised brow. But he was neither bleeding nor dreaming, and the slip and lurch of his horse shook him back to himself. It was the stalings and droppings on the flagstones underfoot that the creature had slipped on. He was in a pillared aisle, looking under a pointed arch, at an interior that reeked like a mistal and was noisy with human voices and lowings. The stone pillars to right and left of him had iron rings let into them, and to one of these the Duke, who had dismounted, was tying his horse. Above the ring, from a hook that had been driven into the crack of a capital, hung a feed of hay in a rope net. The stone flagging of the floor was chipped and cracked with the stamping of horses, and where the feet of dead-and-gone worshippers had worn a shallow channel rivulets of micturition trickled or stood in pools. He felt the stirrup-ropes being loosed from his feet, together with extra cords, for he had been less free to leap from the saddle than he had thought, and again a jog in the ribs told him to descend. As he slid to the ground he saw the opposite aisle across the nave, with its clerestory above it. The lower part of the church was warm with firelight, but above was still a rolling of mists, for of the clerestory glass not a pane remained, and the roof could scarcely be seen. He was thrust forward into the nave, where he stood looking stupidly at the dreadful desecration about him.

Yet he had only to cast his thoughts back and there was nothing to wonder at. Long ago, as a boy, he had been sent to the Saltings, where Roger the smuggler landed his wares and his shore-agent had his depôt. Thither the men of the region had repaired for the contraband, and Roger's office was a hut built into a mudbank, outside which his hoy had lain bilge-keeled till the return of the tide. Just so it must be here. Here, too, hidden in the fog, was the landing-place with its jetty and barges, with Intake's church to serve for warehouse. Axes had been taken to the pews and woodwork to make a clearance. Stall-ends and benching, poppyheads and broken sedilia leaned against pillar and wall, and of these they made their fire that burned on the ground in front of the altar. Here, too, they held their mart. Unopened bales and cases blocked the arches, kegs and drums and jars and bottles were heaped where the pews had been. The straw of broken packages littered the place, and not only the barges brought the loot, but the despoiling of a dozen pack-trains was also to be seen. Clothing and finery hung from cords slung from pillar to pillar. Harness had been flung down in heaps among the hams and flitches in their cloths, the ginger and preserves in their baskets, cheeses from Holland, Italian sausages, dried fruits from Alicant. Looking towards the fire, Robyn saw that a man was toasting cheese at it, two others were smoking tobacco, and in place of the holy vessels bottles and drinking-cups turned the altar into an inn-table.

And in recesses that he could not see, beasts tugged at their rings, and now and then a dog growled, and the fog poured in at the broken clerestory, and the fire leaped into fresh flames as a man cast on it a piece of oak carved with an angel's head. Then Robyn's eyes, rising, saw a marble tablet on a wall. What name had formerly been carved in that chaste and pious marble he did not know, but he saw what was on it now. It had been filled in and whitened over, and under a funeral-urn had been painted on it instead, in gross black, the name of the Earl of Hornsea.

Quite quietly, he was musing now. The Earl of Hornsea. That was the one who had lingered on, but had presently died and been shovelled into a grave; but these had come with a kelp-cart, and carried him away again, and set his memorial up here. For all Robyn knew they had reburied him here, but none of it made much difference now. There was no faintest hope of escape, and with that he began to look more particularly at his captors.

In such fantastic surroundings it was difficult to count them, but they could hardly have been fewer than fifty or sixty. He wondered that they should be so many, but in the same moment his wonder died away again. It was his time, not her own, that the Princess Moggy had been wasting at that fatal halting-place of an inn. Where the first word had come from he did not know, but he knew now that even while his teal had been cooking, and he had taken his short walk as far as the Woolpack and the market-cross, the news of his arrival had already been on its way. Horses had been mounted as he had supped, and the men had looked in to note his face, and had stolen into the kitchen to make their hurried plans, and there was no more need to guess who this dying mother was to whom he had begun his unfinished letter. She was Peg Fyfe, the Queen Herself, and these now gathered to judge him were her spawning and their kin. From the desolate places beyond Mocklington they had ridden in, from the marshes of Humber and North Cave, and the storehouse-church must have its guard and garrison too, for over in a transept he saw pallet-beds and clothing, and others were eating their suppers at the altar-fire now.

The rest were the refuse of the wars, the deserters from this powerful man's retinue or that, the rabble who knew no duty but to save their skins, and what mercy could he hope for here? Already they were bestirring themselves. The chancel was a bustle of men carrying chairs and benches. Two of them were carrying in two thrones, which thev set up behind the altar. Preparations were being made at the back of the church too, and the men and their morts were settling themselves among the wares, and a sort of barrier was being set up across the nave, as they converted it into a dock.

But through Robyn's head a procession of other churches now seemed to be passing – Mixton, where the knight and the lady lay so still on their table of stone – Umpleby and its unresting minster-chimes – Mocklington's lacy spire that swung twelve foot in the wind – stately York, where he had begun to learn his trade —

But at the thought of the half-octagon of an open-air pulpit, with a stairway from an unfinished chapel, up which the curate of the place had mounted to preach to the household and tenantry assembled on the lawns below – at this thought he closed his eyes.

Suddenly there sounded through the church three blasts of a horn. They were evidently an assembly-call, for there was a general stir of making ready. Two men with halberds advanced to the bar across the nave. At the back of the church men and their morts and concubines pressed forward, finding for themselves stations among the wares and between the arches of the aisles, and into the dock were marched two hangdog-looking fellows and a drab of a woman.

But on Robyn a more special attention was bestowed. A chair was placed for him half-way between the dock and the altar, and into it he was thrust. As again the horn was heard there stepped forward the man who had sounded it.

He wore a tabard like a herald, and from the altar end he raised a hoarsely commanding voice.

'Rise for His Grace the Lord Chief Prognosticator!' he ranted, and slowly there made its way from the chancel to the altar a short procession, first two acolytes, then an almoner in a pair of soiled white gloves carrying a parchment on a cushion, and then a lean fantastic figure in a steeple hat trimmed with fur, a furred robe and a long black wand in his hand. He in his turn was followed by the Duke of Spurn, ermined and coronetted again, leading the crimson-turbaned Moggy by the hand. These placed themselves on the two thrones behind the altar, and to right and left of them there ranged themselves some six or eight others, in solemn fool's-coats and chains of office, stolen from heaven knew where. Again the horn sounded thrice and the herald retired. Only the Prognosticator remained standing, and Robyn could see that under his steeple hat hung thin straight wisps of grey hair, and that he had a crafty and lawyer-like face, and as plainly as if he had been there he heard Hendryk's voice again, describing some civil-spoken man who had once offered to carry a letter. 'That's his clothes, not him,' Robyn had commented saucily when Hendryk had finished with his fur cap and fur-lined boots and other indications that he was a person of repute. But this same man – for who else could it be? – had now taken the parchment from the cushion, and stood with it unrolled in his hand as he read aloud in a high and nasal and official voice.

Dully Robyn watched the hugger-mugger from his chair in the middle of the nave. The parchment had a fringe of seal-bags dangling from its lower border, and purported to be some sort of a Charter, by virtue of which the grantees and their assigns enjoyed the right to protect their weaker neighbours from molestation and harm, in consideration of which protection tribute and a fee were authorized and licensed. It was full of solemn mumbo-jumbo and repetitions of meaningless phrases, for rapacity and plunder ever mask themselves with such tarnished trimmings and trappings, though their broken seals are no more than fragments of old wax in their dusty bags. Ask Watty the kempery-man how long it is before that faded licence becomes a banditry of its own, if indeed licence had even been granted at all. But Robyn was watching those idiot seals, dangling from the parchment's edge as if the traitors in York had come to life again and were wagging their heads on their windy spikes. Why were they wasting time over all this rigmarole? They knew what they were here for, and Robyn knew it too.

But the shout that went up when the reading came to an end was its own warrant. Replacing the parchment on its cushion, the reader stood looking round the church and congregation. His formal office discharged, his voice was heard again, on an easier level. He was telling them that if by their Charter it was their duty to protect others it was no less their duty to protect themselves, and unhappily their sovereign lady to whom they all owed allegiance was prevented from being present at her own High Court. She did not, however, go unrepresented, for – and stepping aside he made a sweeping reverence to the Princess Moggy and the Regent Duke, who stiffened suddenly on their thrones.

With these formalities the Court was now in session.

The Prognosticator appeared to be the Prosecutor too, but it was plain that judgement rested with the ermined Duke and the turbaned Moggy. As some form of charge was read out, Robyn heard movements behind him, for the three who sat between the halberdiers were to be disposed of first. The steeple-hatted lawyer, taking up his place at the altar end, was making balancing movements with his hands, now this hand, now that, as he addressed first the tribunal, then the accused. And suddenly Robyn ceased to find anything ludicrous in their tawdy array, for judgement was summary, sentence executed upon the spot. He did not look round, but harsh words of admonition told him that one of the prisoners was being discharged. After a few brief questions the woman, too, was bidden to stand aside, but the third man was not so fortunate. His crime, Robyn vaguely gathered, was that of robbing a fellow-thief, and for this he was ordered a flogging. As somewhere a horse was loosed from its ring and the man tied to the pillar in its place the Duke on his throne adjusted his coronet to another angle and straightened his ermined tippet. But as the first stroke descended and a high howl followed it the eyes of the dwarf who had cooked Robyn's teal took on a new gleam. They were fixed first on Robyn's, and then behind him, as if they scanned some horizon for farther-fetched cruelties, not to be visited on common misdemeanants. The punishment ended. The bar behind Robyn was removed and the halberded gaolers brought their chairs forward. Robyn now sat between them. The preliminaries were over.

Yet they could not begin without another miming, that again needed the services of an acolyte. Surpliced now over his ragged clothing, he carried an open book on a patina, which the Prosecutor took in his hand. His hanks of grey hair shone rusty in the firelight as he turned his head this way and that, gathering their attention. His thin lips seemed to be tasting their own spittle and his eyes flickered here and there like darts as he prepared to read.

But he had not read ten words before Robyn's thoughts had taken a flight far, far from that desecrated church, half a life back from that moment of time. He was at Unthank again, and that afternoon Watty the fenman had called to see John Skyrme. Robyn had been told to go up to his belfry chamber and fetch the great rushlight-scorched Bible, and it was not the Prosecutor, but he himself who was reading out the words, while John and Watty exchanged glances on the settle:

'And if any mischief follow, then thou shalt give life for life, eye for eye, tooth for tooth, hand for hand, foot for foot, burning for burning, wound for wound, stripe for stripe – '

Over the press of faces he saw the marble tablet on the wall, with the name of the Earl of Hornsea written on it in black. Turning the other way he saw a second tablet facing it, but this time the name was the name of the Prince of Withernsea.

For whispering a few words in Starlight's ear this was the retribution they had stored up for him.

And he also knew, such was their mocking deference to observances, that if he had demanded that one should speak for him and be his friend they might have granted him the shadow of it, but what would it have availed him? Let them do their worst, he could still laugh the last. He was bidden to stand up, and he stood up. He was ordered to answer the questions briefly, and he answered them briefly.

'What,' the rasping voice asked, 'is your name?'

'Robyn Skyrme.'

'Was Skyrme also your father's name?'

'Yes.'

'Have you ever travelled from place to place under any other name?'

'Yes.'

'Under what other name?'

'Robyn Waygood.'

'Is that the name you are at present known by?'

'Yes.'

'Where have you lately come from?'

'From York and places near York.'

'By what name were you known there?'

'Skyrme.'

'When did you cease to call yourself by the name of Skyrme and take the name of Waygood?'

'When I began to get near Holderness,' and the furred speaker turned his head in an aside to the Duke of Spurn and his sister Moggy.

'As he approached your royal mother's domain he found it expedient to travel under another name.' Then, turning to Robyn again, 'For what reason did you assume this name of Waygood, that was not your own?'

'I heard of others calling themselves by names that are not their own.'

'A pert answer. It shall be dealt with. What is your trade?'

'I am a mason.'

'Were you ever employed at a place called Mocklington?'

'Yes.'

'By what name were you known there?' Then, as Robyn hesitated, 'Skyrme?'

'No.'

'Waygood?'

'No. I have forgotten,' and again the lawyer addressed Moggy and the Duke.

'He cannot remember all his names.' Then suddenly, 'Have you ever called yourself Richard Eccles?'

'Yes,' said Robyn, now that it had come almost welcoming the name he had striven to remember.

'At Mocklington?'

'Yes.'

'The information before the Court is that you are on your way to seek work there again. Would it not be a disadvantage to do this, having forgotten the name you went by before?'

'Yes.'

'They would wonder? They would ask questions?'

'I should answer them,' and the lawyer turned over a paper.

'To what branch of your Guild are you affiliated?'

'I do not belong to any Guild,' and again the Prosecutor turned to the two who nodded clownishly on their thrones.

'He claims to be a mason, but he does not belong to any Guild. He is seeking work, but cannot remember which of his names he last worked under, and he answers the Court rebelliously.' Then, once more to Robyn, 'Where were you born?'

'I think at an inn in Lincoln.'

'He thinks he was born in an inn in Lincoln. But at least you know where you spent your early years?'

'It was at a place called Unthank, also in Lincolnshire.'

'Were you there learning to be a mason?'

'No, a farmer.'

'Were you Waygood there, or Eccles?'

'Skyrme. Can I have a drink of water?'

He was given a drink of water, and as first he sipped it and then swallowed it at a gulp he heard his tormentor's voice, speaking to his judges.

'May I suggest, your Highnesses, that he assumed the name of Waygood hoping that it might make the *way good* for him?'

At this sally the Duke was suddenly seen to be convulsed with laughter, in which the rest of the bench joined him. He laughed till his eyes were wet with tears, and the lawyer had to quell the merriment that ran contagiously through the Court. But the dwarf in the turban only sat on her twitching hand to keep it still, and again gazed away over Robyn's head. Order was restored and the questioning was resumed.

'So you spent your early days in Lincolnshire. Do you know a place called the Saltings, a few miles south of a place they call the Point or Spit?'

'Yes.'

'When were you last there?'

'I think about seven years ago.'

'He thinks about seven years ago. And do you remember any occasion – any *particular* occasion – on which the peace of this place was violently disturbed?'

'I think I know the time you mean,' said Robyn.

'Will you tell their Highnesses and the Court what that occasion was?' And as Robyn did not answer he helped him out. 'For example, it is said that those of the neighbourhood were given to a form of trading, not open and lawful, such as you have heard described in our Charter, but – in short – smuggling?'

'I've heard tales,' said Robyn.

'And having heard tales, did you ever consider it your duty to lay an information before the properly constituted authorities?'

'No,' said Robyn.

'On the contrary, you yourself were once apprehended by the officers of this august Court, with a pack of liquor on your back, actually assisting in this unlawful traffic?'

Robyn did not reply.

'Come, come,' and Robyn's eyes followed the finger that pointed suddenly to the altar. The drinking vessels had been cleared away, and there stood his pack with its contents set out beside it, his clothing, his tools, his ink-horn and paper, Hendryk's unopened flask of schiedam. The Prognosticator's voice rose.

'And on the following night there was a deplorable affray in this same neighbourhood of Unthank, in which the properly appointed collectors were set upon in the execution of their right and duty – set upon by a treacherous ambush, and shots were fired, and an exalted personage died on the spot, and another was grievously wounded and the rest compelled to retire?'

'I wasn't there,' Robyn said faintly.

'Do you mean that by that time you had left Unthank to seek your fortune elsewhere?'

'I wasn't in Hagthorpe Lane,' and a growl ran through the church as the Prosecutor threw up his hands in their furred sleeves.

'Your Royal Highness hears that? That he wasn't in Hagthorpe Lane? Did *I* speak of Hagthorpe Lane? Did any in this Court mention Hagthorpe Lane? Is there any Hagthorpe Lane in the pleadings? Is there anything about Hagthorpe Lane *there*, or *there*?' And this time the arm shot out first to one of the two wall-tablets, then to the other. Then his voice became sardonic. 'But stay. He is a mason. Memorials are his trade, and he has confessed he is looking for work. Perhaps he would add to the name of our late Lord that he died in Hagthorpe Lane! Order!' for again the growl had run through the church, and the faces had pressed forward between the pillars, and two men behind Robyn were restraining a woman, who was trying to break forward. 'This Court is not a mummers' booth! He has told us that he was not in Hagthorpe Lane that night! Let him now tell us that he was not in Hagthorpe Lane the night before! Perkyn!' And at the call there rose at the other end of the altar the death's-head-looking fellow whose voice, but not his face, Robyn had remembered in the inn. 'Is your name Perkyn?'

'Yes, your Grace.'

'Have you two other names that you doff and don to suit the company you are in?'

'No, your Grace. Only Perkyn.'

'Are you a sworn member of our Brotherhood?'

'Yes, your Grace.'

'Then the Court needs no other oath. Have you ever seen the accused before?'

'Yes, your Grace.'

'Be so good as to tell the Court when and where.'

But Robyn hardly heard them now. He was no longer thinking of that evening long ago when he had been suddenly set upon, and carried away into the sandhills, and the point of a knife had been set to his throat, and he had received orders that Unthank's four best horses were to be under the yew trees at eight o'clock the following evening, with halters and their feed round their necks, in which he would fail at his peril. His peril was here, but his deliverance was here too, not a lad's pistol carved out of an old holly-root, but an engine of mercy and despatch, loaded with ball and its priming seen to only a few hours before. In the past, when he had read aloud to Sim Dacres from the Register and the Book of Martyrs, Sim had told him that even the Smithfield saints had been allowed their bags of gunpowder to shorten their sufferings, and his prayer was that his pistol would do its work without missing, for he had seen the preparations at the altar table.

Irons, and the fire on the ground, and Moggy Fyfe's eyes, now on Perkyn, now on himself. He would lie on no quiet stone slab in an aisle, with a lady with her garter on her arm sleeping placidly by his side. Again he glanced at those infamous tablets on the wall, while fragments of question and answer passed by his ears.

'You say he had been drinking heavily?'

'He was that drunk he could hardly stand, your Grace.'

'So young, and already a graceless reprobate! And was he addressed by our late Lord in due and proper form and told what was required of him?'

'Aye, he was warned proper.'

'The Prince, as became his station, used no violence?'

'It was me just touched him with the knife, your Grace.'

'Merely in the salutory sense, that in recalcitrant cases our form requires?'

'As your Grace says.'

Again the voices died away. They died as that brief and passing beauty of his own life had died, and he would have felt for his pistol there and then but feared to betray his possession of it. Who knew but in that red flash from a muzzle, that twinkling of an eye that is to change us all, the fullness of all beauty might not lie? Perkyn was ordered to stand down. Fierce eyes were on him, for the cattle moving and munching in the aisles had the gentlest hearts there, and there was the chill of death in the very next question that was put to him.

'Were you at Unthank on the night when the old pedlar was found?'

'Go away,' Robyn muttered moodily to himself.

'When the ricks were burned?'

'Let me alone,' said Robyn, half asleep.

'And when you returned to Unthank, what did you expect to find there?'

Robyn caught his breath, but did not speak.

'There is no Unthank now.'

'That's what you'd like me to believe,' said Robyn drowsily.

'It was burnt to the ground, and all in it,' but Robyn threw up his head.

'It wasn't burnt to the ground, because you can't burn flints, and it isn't true, because they are better men there than you are.' And as the palsied hand that had cooked his supper shot up, with a pair of iron pincers in it, his own hand stole quietly to the back of his belt.

'Cold!' she screamed. 'Start him with it cold! Tie him and bring him up here!' And the fire was stirred to life and from the aisles there was a breathless surge forward. Robyn felt the grip of the guard on his left.

But not that of the gaoler on his right, for he was ready. No more faith or unfaith, cowardice or courage, reality or dream, golden glimpse or leaden failure. There was a flash, a report, and his hour was over. He had had it in a cornfield, before the moon began to wane.

So, too, glimmers out the wick behind its tallowy horn. At this distance of time the story has taken on other shapes, but that seven years went by between the first threat and the final fulfilment is common to them all, and it is not the setting out that matters, nor even the home-coming, but the journey in between. In the chapel at Maske, with nine plain capitals to bear it company, a stone squirrel still wrings the water from its tail, so leave it so, the record of one who had a cradle, but no grave.

Wherefore, my pretty Robyn, wherever you are, and whoever is with you, fare you well.